Immortal Descent Copyright 2013 Julie Milillo

Book 2 of The Immortal Sin Trilogy

For more information:

www.juliemilillo.com

Cover Design/Images by C & K Creations

Headshot Photography by Amanda Dolly Photography

Immortal Descent – Book 2 of The Immortal Sin Trilogy

ISBN: 1492220973

ISBN 13: 9781492220978

Library of Congress Control Number: 2013916161

CreateSpace Independent Publishing Platform

North Charleston, South Carolina

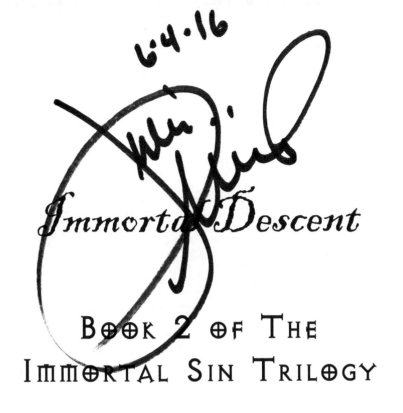

Immortal Descent

BOOK 2 OF THE
IMMORTAL SIN TRILOGY

IF YOU LOST CONTROL,
HOW FAR WOULD YOU FALL
TO MAKE THINGS RIGHT?

Julie Milillo

Acknowledgements

I would like to thank all of my family and friends for their unconditional love and support!

A special thank you:

Editor, Belle Burr

Photographer, Amanda Dolly

Pendant/Jewelry Designer, Rosie Laughlin

Artist, Kris Night

And my husband, Michael for always being there for me and believing in me.

I love you.

For my brother,

Mitchell

Darkness is a difficult thing to overcome but I know there is light within you.

I have faith in you and I will always be here for you.

Stay strong and I love you.

I don't know what I would do without you in my life.

"Those whom we most love are often the most alien to us."

Christopher Paolini, *Eldest*

"She can feel his blood, just beneath his skin; when he breathes, the air fills with smoke. He's like a dragon, ancient and fearless."

Alice Hoffman, *Here on Earth*

"To see a candle's light one must take it into a dark place."

Ursula K. Le Guin

"You're gonna see things you might not wanna see.

It's still not that easy for me, underneath."

– Adam Lambert

"When you feel my heat, look into my eyes. It's where my demons hide, it's where my demons hide. Don't get too close, it's dark inside. It's where my demons hide, it's where my demons hide."

– Imagine Dragons

"Everybody's got a dark side. Do you love me? Can you love mine? Nobody's a picture perfect, but we're worth it. You know that we're worth it. Will you love me? Even with my dark side?"

-Kelly Clarkson

CHAPTER INDEX

Chapter 1

TR⊕UBLE MAKER

*T*he hazy street lights formed what appeared to be a halo glowing from behind his head in the warm air of the dark summer night.

Her Malicious. Her Mitch.

Amanda looked up at him from the floor of the car and their eyes connected. Ironically enough, he was the vision of her very own angel, an Angel of Darkness. He was perfect in every way and she was despairingly in love with him.

As she turned and crouched down under the steering wheel, she held the small, delicate wires in the palms of her hands.

Two months had passed since spring break when she had found out the truth about her identity and subsequently; Mitch had officially become her confidant and boyfriend.

Since the moment they had reconciled, he had devoted his every moment to stay by her side. He was determined to protect her and teach her how to control her darkness.

Everything in the past had been forgiven and life had started anew for them both.

Having spent so much time with her Demon boyfriend, she constantly had the strong desire to create mischief and mayhem. She had learned new abilities, including how to move incredibly fast and forming Hellfire from the palms of her hands. Despite the occasional dueling thoughts and headaches, she stayed with Mitch and refused to be with anyone else. Her life had been drastically changing and adapting to the darkness didn't seem so difficult with Mitch by her side.

That was all she needed.

It was the last night of May and spring was transitioning to summer. The warm weekends had become their time to prey on Middleton. It was their own riotous playground, nothing could have been more gratifying but not everyone was too thrilled about it.

Gregg hadn't been too pleased with her spending all of her time with Mitch, but she couldn't help herself.

At times, she felt as if Gregg were trying to overpower her decision making. Amanda understood that she hadn't practiced much of her angelic powers and occasionally, it seemed that a strong force would make her think twice before she acted. But that force she knew very well as the White Light within her and she refused to cooperate with it. Amanda figured that if headaches were all she would have to endure to be with Mitch, then so be it.

When Amanda decided to forgive and forget with Mitch, she hadn't realized it but she had a tendency to belittle anything or anyone else, except Alexia. Amanda never disrespected Alexia and there wasn't any possible way that Alexia would let that happen without Amanda taking an even greater beating from her if she ever did. Alexia was practically her sister and nothing in the universe would ever change that.

Despite how powerful Amanda had become, Alexia didn't let it alter their relationship. Even though they both knew Amanda was something from out of this world, Alexia wasn't going to let her get away without finishing what they had started; specifically graduating high school and going to the senior prom. Amanda had reluctantly promised her friend that she would complete their senior year together even though she knew her future after high school was unknown.

All of it was pointless.

The night air was still and the street was silent as Mitch stood outside the car waiting for Amanda. The impatient tapping of his foot on the pavement seemed to give her the subtle hint that she was taking too long.

She could feel her heart pounding for the satisfying desire of chaos, but just as she was about to ignite the wires, her White Light from within prevented her from going any further. Her hands trembled with anger as she tried to force through the barrier that was freezing her in place.

Not again…

It was a continuous inconvenience when they were out on nights like this one.

The Light…

Amanda clenched her fist tightly as she grew increasingly frustrated. She felt the invisible energy restraining her and she couldn't help but fight back against it. She could feel that force, her angelic power firmly freezing up her hand, preventing her from starting the fire she so desperately wanted to set alight.

A slight pain started to grow in her mind and she knew another headache was certain to happen.

Amanda closed her eyes tightly, trying to regain her focus and after a moment, she finally sparked the wires. Amanda watched them burst into bright flames as her eyes ignited into their supernatural glow.

Amanda quickly let go and glanced to her side at Mitch who was leaning against the open door with an approving smile. He winked at her as he took her hands and lifted her out of the car. Amanda could feel the crunch of glass shards beneath her sneakers as he set her down onto the pavement.

Mitch leaned down and kissed her on her forehead and then on her mouth.

More…

One kiss was never enough.

Mitch took her hand in his and in a flash, the two of them took off down the road and disappeared into the night.

———oℓℓℓℓ———

"Amanda, this has got to stop!"

The first words Amanda heard when she came through the front door were never what she wanted to hear. The past two months of criticism was starting to get a little overwhelming and tiring.

Amanda rolled her eyes and shut the front door behind her as she walked into the small foyer.

Her head was pounding with pressure from her less than normal headaches.

It was well past midnight and it was evident that Nan had been up impatiently waiting for Amanda to get home.

The woman's eyes were alive with concern despite the dark circles below them.

The Ancient Angel hadn't assumed that it was such a difficult task to just watch over her granddaughter. There had been multiple and more complicated situations that she'd dealt with before yet she never could've predicted the difficulty of watching a teenager dealing with typical attitude issues. However Amanda was after all, more than just an average and typical teenager.

The lectures from Nan had become an ongoing affair after Amanda had made the decision to spend most, if not all of her time with Mitch.

Or as Nan preferred to call him… *the Demon.*

The antique lamp hanging from the ceiling illuminated the foyer, leaving the rest of the house in the shadows.

Nan was standing at the foot of the staircase with her arms crossed and a troubled look on her face. Amanda sighed and glared back at her grandmother before lifting her hands to her temples and rubbing them gently.

"Patience is a virtue, isn't it?" Amanda said sarcastically.

"Don't you preach to me, young lady. You have no idea how worried I've been. This has been going on for too long and it needs to stop right now."

"Nan, please, I don't understand why you can't accept this. I *need* this." Amanda's hands dropped and landed on her hips as she looked away from Nan and in the direction of the living room. Oreo was peeking out from behind the arm of the couch, wide eyed as he watched their debate.

"Darling, I understand you have needs that your Light can't always offer, but this is getting absurd! You're out of control, and this is more serious than you think it is. Amanda, I think car fires are quite extreme and causing accidents that aren't meant to happen is a dangerous thing to trifle with." Nan said.

"Nan…" Amanda said but was interrupted before she could get the chance to talk.

"Don't you remember The List? It's called that specifically for a reason. It's not called *a mess* because it has an order and we are not supposed to interfere with that order. Mitch is being a horrible influence. Do you remember what I told you?"

"Yes, I remember." Amanda said rolling her eyes once again. "Listen, if this is just about Mitch…"

"This is not just about Mitch. And it most certainly appears that you don't remember anything. So, let's go through this once more. The List is carried out by Mephistopheles's Demons. It contains fates that are due to happen and it's not something you can interfere with. It's the only duty that the Underworld is responsible for carrying out. That was part of the deal between Heaven and Hell in order to keep peace on Earth. What they do down there is their business but this is different. Earth is where you meet in the middle, Amanda. It's your haven, your sanctuary and it needs to be protected. You're being hasty and unreasonable. And now that everything is out in the open, we need to be more vigilant and careful."

Nan took a deep breath before continuing to try and clarify the reality of what was happening. Amanda was the Immortal Sin but she was also still a young teenager who had much to learn.

"Nan, you're overreacting." Amanda said in an attempt to interject.

"Can you imagine if you destroyed a life when it wasn't supposed to happen? It is incredibly dangerous to even involve the lives of humans when it is not called for. I know the Amanda I raised would be devastated. It's true that the answer to your fate as the Immortal Sin is still unclear but you still have to abide by certain rules. Being irresponsible is out of the question. We are in hot water as it is right now because the truth's been revealed. Don't you realize that at any given moment anyone, even *you* could be in danger and you don't listen to anyone but that... that Demon!" Nan's voice expressed nothing but disappointment.

"Stop calling him *that*! He has a name!" Amanda snapped. "And of course it sounds bad when you talk about it like that. Trust me. It's not like that and I would never let it go that far!"

"Don't talk to me about trust, Amanda. Do you think making the daily news isn't taking things too far?" Nan asked.

"The news?" Amanda asked, feeling slightly taken back. "I didn't know..."

"Yes, the news! They have been reporting all around this town about the crime that's been being committed and that they have been unable to find the culprits. You didn't know about that because you're too preoccupied with... *him*!"

"I'll do what I want, Nan! I mean, the news thing isn't a big deal. I just can't believe that you don't trust me!" Amanda yelled. The pain in her head continued to grow and the argument certainly wasn't making it any better.

"I think the news thing says it all and it's not a matter of trust right now, Amanda. It's about responsibility for your actions and the results of those actions. Trust can always be rebuilt but it's a matter of that person making an effort to try first. I truly don't think you understand how serious the situation is right now. It is extremely dangerous and who knows what could happen to you or anyone else for that matter! You are acting like a stubborn and naive child. This is not the Amanda I raised!"

"No, I don't think *you* understand, Nan! You have no idea what I'm going through and you never leave me alone about it! All you ever say anymore is *this is not the Amanda I raised. Why don't you have any control? What is wrong with you? You're not thinking!*" Amanda mocked her grandmother. "I'm different now Nan, and you're right, I'm not the Amanda you raised!" Amanda retaliated, harsh words simply shooting out of her mouth with ease.

The moment the words came out, it shocked even her and she knew it would hurt her grandmother, but after she discovered the truth, everything between them just started to decline. Her life was completely different now, and she felt more alone than ever before. Everyone was criticizing her and telling her what to do and what not to do.

For years, Amanda had been grateful for her grandmother and all the things she had done. But there was so much more she hadn't known and important people she had yet to officially get acquainted with. It was incredibly frustrating and all it did was make her heart ache and her head pound.

Nan glared back at her, with an even deeper disapproving expression. Her grandmother was getting exhausted from trying to get Amanda under control. The elderly Angel was growing tired of watching her granddaughter become a menace and quite possibly, a monster.

"It's not all about you, Amanda. There are bigger things at stake here and being careful should be your first priority now that everything is out in the open. You have to understand that your negative attitude is growing. That Demon's energy has been attributing to your decisions and your selfishness has become unrelenting. It's been keeping you from thinking clearly. Do you hear yourself speak? You're much smarter than this." Nan said, once again attempting to explain the reality of the situation.

"Alright, alright! I'm sorry, okay?" Amanda said reluctantly, holding up her hands in surrender.

As stubborn as she was, Amanda couldn't help but further explain her reasoning for her actions.

"I just have these needs and it feels right to do what I want. Besides, you're the one that said it was fine that I spend time with him as long as he's not in the house or on the property. I thought you understood…"

Nan sighed in defeat. The Ancient Angel knew that it was going to be a difficult task to reach out to her teenage granddaughter. She was the Immortal Sin, but she was also still a teenager. It was starting to appear that Amanda was going to have to learn on her own.

"Just go up to your room for the night and promise me that you will try to stop the… mess that you're making around town? We have to be cautious and aware because if Mephistopheles decides to come into the picture, well, he is unpredictable, and he knows how to creep his way in when least expected. Please think about your faith, Amanda, it's very, very important."

"Yeah, yeah. I will, Nan. Thanks." Amanda brushed it off and rolled her eyes, but deep within her heart, she knew that an apology is what she truly owed her grandmother. Nan didn't deserve to be treated the way she'd been dealing with, but she couldn't see any other way to get her point across without laying down the truth.

In the end, she couldn't manage to force the remorseful words out and resorted to the one word that she could.

"Goodnight."

Amanda averted her eyes to the floor, walked past her grandmother and headed up the wooden staircase. She could feel the obnoxious tension between them but chose to ignore it instead of further pressing her luck.

Once Amanda reached her bedroom, she quietly shut the door behind her and kicked off her sneakers.

She plopped down on the soft mattress and looked up at the blank ceiling. She could feel her vast wings flowing off either side of the bed as the tips brushed the wooden floor planks. They remained invisible to the eye but she could always feel them there.

Amanda closed her eyes and tried to calm her negative energy. She sighed with relief when she felt the throbbing in her head begin to subside little by little.

Be reasonable…

Just breathe…

Amanda knew she wasn't behaving like the girl she used to be before everything changed, but she couldn't help it. All the time she'd spent with Mitch had such an influence on her and it was impossible to fight, especially because she enjoyed being around him.

Mitch…

Amanda loved him and why would anyone reject the thought of being without the one person who made you feel… extraordinary?

She craved the sensations that took hold of her whenever she was around him. Amanda felt like a different person, like someone who could just let go of everything and not have a care in the world. The carefree and reckless attitude felt so rapturous and so amazing that it almost seemed like it was too much to handle at times.

More…

She just wanted more and more of it, which led her to assume that was what made a Demon seemingly… evil: the crazed acts of carelessness and the intense hunger for more power.

Greed and selfishness.

Yet despite all of these dark sensations, Mitch still managed to see the light within her. She had managed to show the Demon what love truly was without even realizing it.

Amanda was grateful for that but whenever they were apart, she had moments where she yearned to open up the light from inside and go back to that peaceful, dreamlike state she fell into when using her White Light.

The real truth of using her dark side so frequently was that it was physically exhausting, draining all of the energy out of her. The effort to form such resentful thoughts in her mind quickly drained her. A good night's rest was definitely what she needed.

When it came to sleep, Amanda's dreams had been empty for two months. No long lasting nightmares and nothing but emptiness.

The one dream that she couldn't seem to forget and the last one she could remember was when she had been sucked down through darkness and into a river of blood. The blinding darkness had kept her from recognizing the sticky liquid and she could remember the taste of metal on her tongue. It had felt so real, so consuming. It felt as if the rapid flow were swallowing her whole, until that one moment. The moment when a hand grabbed hold of hers, pulling her up against the flow, enabling her to finally catch her breath.

Who had reached out to save her?

Mitch had said that it hadn't been him, so who could it have been?

Amanda took a deep breath as she recalled the vivid dream. She tried to turn her thoughts in another direction, away from the tempting call of darkness.

She was so still that she could feel her heart beating in her chest. As she exhaled, Amanda could feel the light within her heart brighten at the thought of the one thing she was secretly looking forward to.

Meeting her...

Serenity.

But when would that ever happen?

At times, when alone, Amanda longed to meet and talk with her mother. She didn't do it much, but when Amanda found the chance to be alone and it was quiet, she would pray.

In the months before, Amanda learned from her grandmother that saying a prayer was a way of communicating between Angels, she would take a moment occasionally in an attempt to reach out, but she never knew if she was doing it the right way. She was always too stubborn to ask Nan how do to it properly. Regardless, the prayers always went unanswered but she tried to do it despite having little knowledge.

It had been too long since she and her mother had talked or even seen each other, but she hoped that their next encounter would be soon, given the events that had happened over the past two months.

Amanda was brought back to reality when she smelt the most familiar scent invade the air around her.

That invigorating scent...

Amanda opened her eyes to see his face leaning in above her. Amanda peered into his hypnotizing onyx eyes and smiled, welcoming his presence.

"I thought you'd never come." Amanda said dreamily.

"You know I can't ever leave you." Mitch leaned in and kissed her ever so gently. Their conjoined lips radiated the familiar and warm shade of red.

Mitch had been secretly sneaking into her bedroom whenever the opportunity would arise.

Nan had warned Amanda that he was not allowed on the premises, but they were inseparable and could barely handle so much time without each other.

Their love was unearthly and it was extraordinarily special. There wasn't any way she would reject or deny it. It was wrong of her to disrespect her grandmother but the urge to have him by her side at any moment grew increasingly stronger over the previous months. In her heart, the old Amanda seemed to tell her that what she was doing was wrong; it was inexcusable but the craving of seeing Mitch seemed to override anything that kept her second guessing.

A small sound suddenly came from the bedroom door and before she knew it, Mitch had disappeared right before her. She marveled at how fast he could move in the blink of an eye. He had grown accustomed to hiding when there was a chance that Nan could show up at any given time.

In the flash of a second, her small window was left open leaving the summer breeze blowing into her room.

"Come in." Amanda said and sat up on the bed. She expected Nan to walk in but no one entered.

The small sound came again as if someone had scratched at the wooden door. Amanda walked over and peered out to find Oreo sitting at her feet. She picked up the dog and cradled him in her arms as she peeked down the hallway. The lights were off and Amanda could see that Nan had finally gone to bed.

Amanda shut the door quietly then placed Oreo on her bed.

"You know, sneaking behind your grandmother's back is actually kind of fun. It's like a game."

"A very dangerous game, we really have to be careful." Amanda said, thinking about how her grandmother would react if she ever found out.

"It's kind of… well, what's the term the students use at your school? Some of the girls say it and then the guys say it about the girls? You know, the word that Alexia uses quite often?"

"Hot?" Amanda asked.

"Yea, it's pretty hot." Mitch said, attempting to talk like a normal high school student.

Amanda tried to hold back from bursting with laughter.

"You know, it's a good thing you don't actually go to school with me because other kids might think you're just plain weird." Amanda giggled.

"Oh well."

A smile lit up his face and it made him all the more irresistible.

"You have no idea how silly you look when you say stuff like that." Amanda giggled. "Stick to the stuff you already know, okay?"

"Are you sure? I'm trying. I mean who wouldn't want a slice of this?" Mitch said and gestured to his entire body.

"No, not a *slice* of this. It's a *piece of this.*'" Amanda smiled as she shook her head.

"Oh, that's right! Pizza is slice. Dammit. Little stuff like that still confuses me sometimes." Mitch said. "Alright, I'll stop. But in all seriousness, it's quite impressive that you're going behind your grandmother's back."

"Don't remind me."

Amanda frowned at the thought of her grandmother. All it reminded her of was the negativity she'd been tossing at her and the White Light that she hadn't been working with when she knew she was supposed to. She had occasionally contemplated practicing with her White Light, but she always ended up getting pulled right back into Mitch's deviant yet irresistible arms. And there was no way she was going to feel bad about that.

"Don't worry. Look at it this way, at least I get to spend the night. We get to be with each other. At least we can make the most of that." Mitch said, smiling at her.

Amanda nodded in response as she sat down next to Oreo. She knew he was right. Mitch never actually fell asleep but when he would secretly stay over for the night, he would simply hold her close in his warm embrace. He knew that she needed protection and he was there to provide that for her. True, her grandmother offered protection, maybe even more powerful protection but Mitch *needed* to be there for her, to fight anything that came their way. Nothing could tear them apart.

He loved her. She loved him. It was as simple as that.

However, there was one thing that posed a huge threat to their future and Mitch couldn't help but try to force it from his memory. He could still hear Ravish's ear piercing scream as she had reached out and writhed in agony before she'd been banished by Nan.

The words echoed loudly in his mind and he winced at the words that continued to haunt him.

Malicious, you will pay for what you've done!

It constantly reminded Mitch of the danger that was likely boiling in the pit of Hell, waiting for the proper moment to strike.

Chapter 2

ADAPTATI⊕N

"You know, you really need to stop stealing my stuff." Amanda said, as she watched Mitch pull her MP3 player out from his pocket.

It was a beautiful Saturday afternoon and the early June breeze swept through the meadow. Amanda and Mitch lay in the grass, as she tried to focus on her Math homework.

"I know, but music is just so... addicting." Mitch said, sliding the tiny buds into his ears.

"For the tenth time, they're called *AC/DC*. And you know that there's more than one rock band. You don't have to keep listening to the same one over and over again. And next time, can you ask me first? Or at least tell me when you're taking it, that way I'm not wondering where it is all the time." Amanda smiled before turning her focus back to the thick textbook.

Given the amount of time they had spent together, Mitch had begun adapting to Amanda's human life. She had shown him different types of music and even bought him a cellphone to keep track of his location and communicate when they weren't together.

"Amanda, you know that all of this is pointless." Mitch gestured to the textbook and the backpack she was leaning on. She knew he wasn't accustomed to the average way of life that she had once known but she continued to try and encourage him to go with the flow of how things had to be until school was over with.

"I know, I know but I made a promise to Alexia and I won't... I can't break it. I promised I'd at least finish senior year. She'd kill me if I didn't after all we've been through. I don't care if I'm an Angel, a Demon... or even an alien, I have to do this. It's for her and I won't risk losing our friendship all because of this change." Amanda said.

"It's kind of a big change though." Mitch retorted.

"Yeah, well, it's the least I can do and she's my best friend. I can't hurt her again. I won't do that to her."

"Alright, but do we have to go to that dance thing? What's it called again?"

"Do you mean the Prom?"

"Yeah, that thing. It sounds so dumb and just boring."

"As boring as you think it might be, we are still going."

"But you're not into the whole getting-dressed-up-thing so why should we go?"

"Because that's all part of this promise and it's kind of a big deal to Alexia. I mean, it's *Prom*. It's a highlight of high school and she doesn't want me, or us to miss it. And yes, I'm dragging you with me, whether you like it or not."

"Well, fine I guess but I'm definitely not looking forward to spending time with that..." Mitch paused and made the last minute decision not to criticize her friend, her Watcher, "...Gregg."

His face contorted into a frown as he shifted uncomfortably at the thought.

"You don't have to tell me twice. Listen, I know you don't like him but someone has to help you get dressed for it. And he's the only one who can help you with that anyway. I'm sorry but Alexia will *not* let you go to something like the Prom in just plain black jeans." Amanda said and gestured to his clothes.

"I have to go dress shopping with Alexia and you know how she is." Amanda smiled. "Just go with the flow and before you know it, high school will be over and we won't have to worry about this stuff."

Mitch sighed as if he still didn't completely understand the bond that she shared with Alexia. A promise was a promise and Amanda knew that all her friend wanted was for her to be happy and to not miss out on anything she could regret. But how could he when he had never shared anything with anyone before?

Over the two months that had passed, it had taken some convincing but Mitch had eased his way into the group with Gregg and Alexia.

The tension between Gregg and Mitch was occasionally distracting given their distinct reservations about one another but they were both willing to try and compromise for Amanda's sake.

Amanda looked up from her book, her attention caught by Mitch's horrible attempt at singing. He was rocking his head back and forth to what she recognized as "Back in Black". He sang the lyrics that he knew loudly as the noise blasted from the earphones. His hands moved around in front of him, as if he were trying to play some form of air guitar. Amanda laughed at his gestures and closed the textbook, deciding to give up on the homework as she leaned forward and tried to get his attention.

"Hey, you! Mister Rock Star!" Amanda said above the music.

"What?" Mitch asked a little too loudly as the music continued to play. He stopped the charade and pulled an ear bud out from one of his ears. "What?"

"I think I'm done studying because I can hardly concentrate with the show you're putting on." Amanda teased.

"I'm not putting on a show!" Mitch said defensively. "I just *love* this music!"

"Okay, well, I have an idea. Why don't you just hold onto it for a while? I think you need it more than I do." Amanda said and shoved her book into her backpack.

A big smile appeared on his face and the Demon leaned in as he kissed her deeply. Amanda laughed at his tendency to be so forward, outwardly reminding her of how much he appreciated and cared for her. He was so spontaneous and she loved it. One minute she'd be talking and then the next minute, his lips would be on hers, hushing her quickly and simply taking her breath away.

Mitch leaned in on her, gently forcing Amanda down into the grass as he pressed his lips on hers. She could feel her wings spread out across the ground as Mitch pulled away from her and looked directly into her eyes.

With a single glance, he captivated her very soul without even trying.

The feeling was indescribable, almost euphoric.

Love was truly an amazing miracle to behold and she had it within the darkness in his eyes.

A moment passed before he spoke.

"Do it. I love when you do it," Mitch said with an encouraging smile.

Amanda knew exactly what he was referring to and she closed her eyes, commanding her beautiful inner peace and seductive darkness. Mitch's face lit up when she opened her eyes, revealing her unique paranormal portals. Her eyes swirled with bright white and charcoal black, showing off her ability to control its' power.

"Why do you love it so much?" Amanda giggled in between his soft kisses before he pulled away once again.

"It's just so… you. This is what you really are and I love to see that."

Amanda smiled and kissed him back welcoming the warm sensation they shared.

How could she resist the irresistible Demon's kiss?

Their lips glowed brightly with the familiar red intensity that made her heart flutter.

A beeping sound came from the pocket of Amanda's jeans, interrupting their intimate moment. Mitch leaned back as Amanda reluctantly sat up and pulled out her cell phone.

"It's Alexia," Amanda said as she read the text message. "She and Gregg want to get pizza. She says they want to talk."

"Well, I guess I'll put up with the Watcher today."

"Gregg…" Amanda corrected him.

"Whatever." Mitch said and stood up and outstretched his palm, offering to pull her up to her feet. "Let's go then. At least I'll be getting pizza out of it."

Amanda tossed her backpack over her shoulder and hand in hand, they headed toward her car.

When it came to pizza, Mitch was more than happy to go where it was. From the moment they went to Romano's together, he was hooked.

Nothing stood between him and his pizza; not even his disdain for a Watcher.

Chapter 3

CONFLICTS

The chimes rang out as Amanda and Mitch walked into Romano's. Gregg and Alexia were sitting at a table near the window, sipping on their cans of soda.

"Hey!" Amanda said as they approached the table. "Did you guys order yet?"

Alexia hopped up from the table and gave Amanda a big hug.

"Not yet but Gregg really wants to talk to you guys about something." Alexia said quietly before the three of them sat back down at the table.

Gregg's gaze never left Mitch, watching his every move as the Demon sat down on the opposite side of the table and wrapped his arm around Amanda's shoulders.

Gregg was always on high alert when Mitch was around, and it was understandable but Amanda wished he made an effort to at least try to act somewhat normal.

Once they all placed their orders with the waitress, the four of them sat in silence, waiting for the first person to speak.

"So, what's up, guys? What'd you want to talk about?" Amanda asked, trying to kick-start the conversation.

Gregg leaned back in his chair with his arms crossed when he finally decided to talk.

"I think we need to start taking extra precautions." Gregg finally said.

With only those few words, Amanda knew why he hadn't come right out with it and she knew exactly where the conversation was heading.

An argument was inevitable.

"Gregg, we're not going through this again. Everything is fine and nothing's happened." Amanda said and looked to Mitch for help. Mitch stayed quiet and simply glared back at Gregg, allowing the Watcher to continue his rant.

"Amanda, I think we can all say that you've been a little... reckless lately, and we all know why."

Gregg's brown eyes remained transfixed on Mitch, with an accusatory stare.

Mitch didn't do or say anything.

After realizing Mitch wasn't going to respond, Gregg finally averted his glare to Amanda.

"We can't be too hasty with the situation. With your true identity out in open for almost two months now, no one knows what will happen next. We don't know what kind of action the Underworld or anyone else will take. You need to be more careful." Gregg said and paused. "I've called for backup."

"He's right, Amanda." Alexia said, reluctantly agreeing with Gregg. "Don't get too angry, we just care about you and I think Gregg's right."

Back up?

"Gregg! Alexia! We don't need backup! I have more control now and nothing has happened! And I haven't been... reckless!" Amanda raised her voice with frustration.

"Yes, you have." Gregg objected.

"No, I haven't!"

"Don't you see? Your dark side has been preventing you from making clear decisions and even listening to any advice that Nan tries to give you. I know that the old Amanda is in there and sometimes you show it, but when you spend all of your time together, you seem to lose focus on anything else around you. You're carrying on like a child! Listen to yourself!" Gregg said, trying to maintain his calm composure.

The Watcher took a deep breath before continuing the conversation. The last thing they needed was a fight to break out in the middle of the small pizzeria for all to see.

Gregg glanced over at Alexia who looked back at him with an encouraging expression to continue. After a moment, he leaned forward, leaning his elbows on the table.

"Listen to me. You're so deep in the darkness that you've practically forgotten how to use or even see your White Light. I understand that you're part of both worlds, but you can't forget how to use your White Light! You *have* to…"

"She doesn't *have* to do anything." Mitch interrupted.

Mitch leaned in toward Gregg, challenging him with a threatening look in his eyes.

"In case you've forgotten, I've been here to help her and guide her. As a matter of fact, you should consider yourself lucky because a Watcher would be quite useless in teaching her how the darkness works. Actually, now that I think about it, what does a Watcher do anyway? You're not really all that significant are you?" Mitch taunted.

"Mitch, don't say that." Amanda said knowing that the hurtful comments weren't necessary.

"Don't you dare question my reason for existing, Demon. I'm a Watcher, also known as a son of God. I was created alongside the Angels."

"Alongside, but that's all. You're still not quite one of them, are you?" Mitch snapped, getting caught up in the intensity of the moment.

"It's not your place to express such judgment. The last thing I would let you do is antagonize me and try to tease me with your lies and deception."

"Boys, please. Let's try to keep this civil, okay?" Alexia interjected, laying her hands out on the table.

"Okay, okay." Mitch said calmly and leaned back in his chair before he added his last comment. "She *needs* me. She *needs* darkness."

Even though everything Mitch had said was the truth, Amanda knew he always had to have the last word and that comment kept Gregg coming back to make a point.

Gregg pointed his finger in Mitch's face with conviction.

"Listen here, Demon. The last thing we need is Amanda to be torn apart by evil like that missing finger of yours. Besides, I've known Amanda longer than you have and I know that she is more than capable of making her own choices." Gregg explained.

"Listen, both of you. I don't need either of you to argue over anything having to do with me. I love you both and I know that you both care." Amanda said, taking hold of Mitch's hand and looking at each of them.

"She knows, guys. But let's remember that we are in a pizzeria right now and this is not the place to start a fight. We are all just trying to do the right thing but are seeing it very differently." Alexia said resting her hand on Gregg's thigh.

"Alright, I know I might've been a little… careless recently but it's in my blood, or my soul… or whatever you want to call it." Amanda confessed. "But I can take care of myself and I really don't think we need backup, Gregg."

"Amanda, you are so stubborn sometimes. You have no idea how aggravating it can be." Gregg said.

"Tell me about it." Mitch agreed.

"Are you guys serious? That's the one thing you're both going to agree on? You know I can take care of myself, especially now that I've learned how to control my powers more than I did before." Amanda said.

"Only your dark powers…" Gregg said under his breath.

"Give her a chance, Gregg. She's trying to explain." Alexia said.

"I know, Alexia but there are some things that can't be prevented all by herself." Gregg explained then turned his attention to Amanda. "Amanda, who knows what Mephistopheles has planned? Just because nothing has happened yet, doesn't mean nothing will happen at all. Think about what happened in Sea Grove and that was *only* Ravish's doing. Something will happen sooner or later and I think it's in our best interest that we have more help if anything were to happen. So, I've called for backup. He's…"

"Another Watcher!" Alexia said excitedly before quickly covering her mouth knowing that she shouldn't have said anything.

"Alexia!" Gregg said loudly, surprised by her interruption and looking at her disapprovingly.

"Well, his name is Lucius, but Gregg and the other Watchers call him Luca for short." Alexia continued without stopping.

"Alexia, please, let *me* explain." Gregg said, encouraging her to stay quiet.

"I'm sorry! But I think this stuff is just so cool and I wanted to be the one to say it! I won't say any more, I promise." Alexia said timidly and pretended to pull an invisible zipper across her mouth.

"...*another Watcher?*" Mitch asked as his facial expression suggested that he'd eaten something rotten.

Amanda didn't feel so confident about the situation either but there wasn't much that could be done about it. She understood that her friends wanted to protect her even if she didn't agree with how they were doing it.

"Yes, *another Watcher.*" Gregg retorted. "He'll be here tomorrow and I told him to meet us over at Sea Grove. And I think it'd be better if only you came, Amanda."

"Oh, come on, Mitch can come if he wants." Alexia said, throwing a friendly wink at Mitch. Alexia never had any qualms with Mitch and she was more than happy to accept him into the group, especially as Amanda's first boyfriend.

Mitch smirked and glared across the table at Gregg.

"Thanks, but no thanks any way. I'd be more than happy to satisfy Gregg's request in not being there. I think it'd make it easier for the both of us if I didn't come." Mitch said and looked over at Amanda. "It'll be easier."

"Are you sure?" Amanda asked, knowing all too well that she wanted Mitch to be there with her.

"Yeah, the one thing I won't fight with him about is your protection, even though I have grown to *despise* Watchers." Mitch winced at the thought of being away from her. "You go ahead and I'll meet up with you later on."

"Good! Now, that we've settled that, and we are all on good terms for now, we can eat! I'm starving!" Alexia said as the waitress approached the table with their orders. Mitch's face lit up as he eagerly reached for his plate, anxious to eat his beloved pizza.

Amanda picked up her slice and took a bite as she thought about what would transpire the next day.

Another Watcher… great.

Chapter 4

LUCA

The warmth from the sun and sound of the waves crashing on the shore seemed to soothe her mind. Amanda looked out at the horizon as she wondered what Mitch was up to. She assumed he was sitting in their field, listening to her MP3 player as usual and messing around with his cell phone.

Mitch didn't understand the concept of having a communication device at first, considering Demons never dealt with such a thing before. But Amanda insisted that he should have one, that way they could always contact each other when they were parted. She had taught him how to send a text message, make a phone call, and even download games to keep him entertained when he couldn't practice his patience.

A small beeping sound came from her phone, disturbing her thoughts. Amanda slid it out from the pocket of her shorts, surprised to find a text message from Mitch.

The sooner u get back, the sooner we can have fun. ;-)
Miss u already.

A nudge came from her side and Alexia stood up from the bench as Amanda slid her phone into the pocket of her capri pants.

"They should be here any minute." Alexia said, biting her lip and adjusting her yellow dress in various places.

On the outside, Alexia appeared to be perfectly collected, but Amanda could tell that she was slightly high strung, as if she were nervous.

"Are you alright? Haven't you met the new one already?" Amanda asked, standing up beside her friend. She didn't see what the big deal was. It was only another Watcher and it wasn't all that fascinating to her that she was going to meet another one that was probably just like Gregg.

Good intentions, but constantly hovering and overwhelmingly protective.

It was hard to believe how much Gregg had changed after the truth had come out. Gregg's once goofy and typical jock-like personality had only been a fake for the past few years she had known him. Little did she know that he was something utterly different the entire time before.

"Not in person or anything, just over the phone. He has a good sense of humor and sounded really cool. A sense of humor is definitely something we need around here lately. Every thing's been so tense it's making me sick." Alexia said.

Amanda could see that her friend was trying as hard as she could to hold back her excitement when suddenly, Alexia busted at the seams.

"This is just so... exciting! I mean getting involved with all this crazy stuff. I know it's been a while that I've known about it but it's still so... unreal! It's like we're in a movie or something! And now I'm meeting *another* Watcher! It's like the stuff you read about when you're growing up. I can only imagine what other things are out there." Alexia said, smiling from ear to ear.

"Just remember that this stays between only us, okay?" Amanda asked.

"Oh, I know. Trust me." Alexia said reassuringly.

At times, Amanda wondered if it would've been a better idea to have kept Alexia in the dark but when Alexia had stumbled upon everything that had happened, there was no turning back. She loved her best friend, but sometimes Alexia was a little difficult to trust. When her excitement would overload, she had a tendency not to pay attention or accidentally let something slip.

As much as Amanda loved telling her friend everything, this new life was going to be even more complicated having already involved Alexia when they didn't have a choice. All of their lives had changed and this new life wasn't like anything they had ever known before.

"Hey, babe."

Gregg's voice came from behind them and Gregg wrapped his arms around Alexia's shoulders, hugging her tightly.

Amanda turned to find the new Watcher standing beside Gregg.

Amanda's mouthed dropped slightly when she first looked up at him. The new Watcher wasn't at all what she had expected.

The feature that stood out the most was his deep blue eyes that seemed to penetrate right through her. He also appeared to be about the same age and he was tall, fit and lean as opposed to Gregg's robust figure. His dirty blonde hair was perfectly parted and it was as if he stepped right out of a magazine cover.

The Watcher's aura seemed very different from Gregg's in that he seemed very down to earth and simple. It gave Amanda a sense of calm, almost like that of Nan's ability whenever she was around her.

"Amanda, this is Luca. Luca, Amanda." Gregg gestured, introducing them to each other.

Amanda hesitated, not knowing what to do or what to say. She seemed to be at a loss for words because she hadn't known what to expect. She'd been so stubborn that she had been caught off guard.

He's just another Watcher…

But before anyone could say a word, Alexia slipped out from under Gregg's arms and stepped in front of Amanda. She extended her palm with a big smile.

"I'm Alexia. I talked to you on the phone the other day." Alexia said, beaming.

"Yes, I figured. Nice to meet you," Luca said smiling, appearing to be amused by her enthusiasm.

Even his voice was smooth and his tone was charming and polite, nothing like she had been accustomed to over the past two months. It was as if he were a breath of fresh air, reminding her how much she actually missed her way of life when using her White Light.

Amanda swallowed hard when she saw his sapphire eyes shift past Alexia and gaze directly at her.

Say something...

"Hi." Amanda managed to squeeze out as Alexia moved aside, tossing her an encouraging look.

"Hi. It's nice to finally meet you. I've heard a lot about you."

"You have?" Amanda asked shyly.

"Of course, you're the Immortal Sin. Everyone knows now and you're friends told me all about you." Luca explained.

"...*All* about me?" Amanda asked, glancing over toward her friends.

Gregg cleared his throat before speaking, in an attempt to change the subject.

"Well, I think we should go for a walk, what do you say?"

"Uh, sure." Amanda raised her eye brows suspiciously toward Gregg.

What exactly did Gregg tell Luca?

"I think you two should get to know each other more now that Luca will be around for a while." Gregg said.

Get to know him?!

First of all, she wasn't a child that needed to be looked after or babysat. Second, wasn't this only supposed to be an introduction?

Amanda crossed her arms uncomfortably and shifted her balance from one leg to the other, trying to decide what she was going to say. She could feel her anxiety building up and the last thing she wanted was to burst into a tirade right on the boardwalk in public.

Before Amanda could say anything, Alexia took Amanda's arm in hers and playfully forced her to walk ahead of Gregg and Luca.

"Come on, Amanda, it'll be fun. Don't start *that* again, *Miss Stubborn*. He's just trying to help out." Alexia said encouragingly. "Just give it a chance, what could it hurt?"

Amanda reluctantly walked ahead, arm in arm with her best friend, leaving the Watchers to follow behind them.

One chance couldn't hurt . . . could it?

Amanda refused to make eye contact with the Watcher. She knew she was being incredibly stubborn but all she wanted at that moment was to go see Mitch.

The four of them sat at a wooden picnic table on the boardwalk, drinking their sodas, eating hot dogs and French fries. Luca sat opposite Amanda, making it even harder for her to avoid him.

"So, what are we up against?" Luca asked.

"Well, like I said on the phone, it's been too quiet. That night I told you about, when that Demon girl found out what Amanda was, well, that's the reason why you're here. That's also when this one found out what was really going on." Gregg said and looked over at Alexia.

"Yeah, that's when I saw *everything*. That was a pretty scary night, one that none of us will forget." Alexia said before taking a sip of her soda.

"How long has it been? When did it happen?" Luca asked, taking a bite out of his hot dog, leaving behind a drop of mustard on his lip.

If there was anything that Amanda learned about Watchers, it was that they loved to eat and they definitely didn't care about the mess they made.

"It's been about two months and I think something's up. I think that Demon, Radish or whatever her name was, is more than likely planning something."

"Ravish, not Radish. What kind of a Demon would be called Radish?" Amanda corrected Gregg.

Alexia almost spit out her soda when she started laughing.

"That'd be interesting, wouldn't it?" Luca said and laughed as he continued his thought, taking advantage of the opportunity to lighten the mood. "Radish, the Demon? You think she'd come after us with something ridiculous, like flaming vegetables?"

Everyone laughed at the joke except Amanda. As a matter of fact, Amanda didn't think it was funny at all. She frowned and crossed her arms, waiting for the conversation to become serious once again.

"Okay, okay. I meant Ravish. A Demon is a Demon, I really don't care about their names. But, anyway, Mephistopheles could be forming some sort of attack as well. They know too much now and we can't be too careful. Amanda needs more protection." Gregg explained.

Amanda huffed in annoyance as she shoved a French fry in her mouth.

"What's wrong, Amanda?" Luca asked, looking up from his food.

Amanda refused to say anything.

"She doesn't feel like she needs protection. She thinks she's strong enough to do *everything on her own*. But it's the Demon I told you about that's influencing her... immoral behavior. I know you don't like hearing it, Amanda, but it's true."

Alexia nudged Gregg in an attempt to be a little nicer about the situation.

"Amanda's independent and she knows what she wants, that's all. I don't think it's all because of Mitch and I know her better than anybody, right?" Alexia said, waiting for Amanda to respond.

Amanda simply nodded her head, confirming that her friend was right.

"And even though she can be stubborn, she fights for what she wants. It's how she's always been. Am I right?" Alexia asked, turning again to Amanda.

"Yeah, you're right." Amanda said, agreeing with her friend even though she knew Gregg didn't entirely understand.

"Well, I admire that." Luca said, smiling at Amanda. Amanda felt the corners of her mouth upturn into a shy grin at the unexpected but uplifting compliment. "May I shed some light on the situation?"

Amanda was willing to listen despite the negativity that was being thrown at her. It was the first time in a while that someone other than Alexia was supporting her way of thinking.

"Don't encourage her, Luca. She needs to work with her White Light before she forgets how to use it." Gregg said, finishing his second hotdog.

"I *won't* forget." Amanda retaliated.

"No, really, I think it's important to stand for what you believe in and what you want. I understand that at times, it can be difficult but sometimes distractions can lead you astray." Luca said with an encouraging smile. "We're just here to help and guide you. Just remember that balance is always a key element, especially in your situation."

"What do you mean *my* situation?" Amanda asked defensively, slightly offended by the comment.

"Well, Gregg told me that you haven't had contact with your real parents in a long time. They're the ones you need to talk to and you have no way of getting to them. I figure once you get some closure or whatever you need from them, at least you'll be able to have a better understanding of what you are and what you're capable of. Balance is the key and with you belonging to two worlds that are very powerful, well, it's really important to be conscientious of that. It's best to have better control and a good balance of both, since you are able to." Luca explained sincerely. "It's good to stand your ground but getting the answers you need is important."

Amanda looked at him in awe. It was as if he met somewhere between Gregg and Mitch with his honesty yet he had respect for what she was trying to do. He understood that she wanted more than anything to be independent but his points went along with exactly that. His pure honesty and words hit her harder than she expected. Amanda hadn't given any thought about how the absence of her parents could be influencing her actions. His words lingered in the back of her mind as they finished up the rest of lunch in silence.

Luca was right.

Could she really be acting up because she wanted more than anything to get the answers that she was missing?

Amanda longed so badly to speak with her parents and Mitch was the only one she felt she could go to for anything. There was always Nan but being kept in the darkness for so many years kind of diminished her belief in her grandmother.

Mitch had enveloped her life in a special comfort, even though that comfort was really darkness.

In addition, there was always a small reminder that would make her think twice about her general make up, also including her actions when she was with Mitch. It had been her dormant White Light the entire time. Amanda had been ignoring it on purpose, letting the darkness override her intuitions, because of her love for Mitch.

It dawned on her that Luca's words were nothing far from the truth. She needed a balance of both light and dark to be more conscious of her actions. The darkness was causing her to act naïve and childish, not like she normally would. Amanda needed a way to make it work equally and stay strong but still find a way to be with Mitch.

She loved Mitch and wanted to spend every waking moment with him, but could he really be some sort of... distraction?

Mitch had told her that she's shown him much more than his hellish existence had ever known.

Could spending too much time with him really be deterring her from thinking clearly and making the decisions she truly wanted?

Chapter 5

HEARTACHE

*L*ater that day, Amanda had driven straight home from the boardwalk. She suddenly felt distant from the rest of the world, and the urge to run straight to Mitch had dissipated.

She was avoiding him and it felt so strange.

Mitch had been texting her, asking her where she was but she refused to answer her phone. She switched the ringer to vibrate, that way the sound wouldn't irritate her. It felt strange to actually consider the fact that Mitch might not be the best thing for her after all.

But they had been through so much together, why a sudden change of heart?

She knew she could never leave him, but maybe some distance was needed to let her try to balance things out, like Luca had recommended.

Without Mitch, learning the darker side of herself could have been much more difficult if she had tried to explore it all on her own. But having known enough about how to control the darkness within her, it was time to move onto her other side, her angelic side. But having learned from the past, in order to do that, space would be needed between she and Mitch in order to attain that knowledge without hurting her beloved Demon.

The love of her life.

The light of the sunset beamed through her bedroom window as Amanda shut the door quietly behind her. She placed her small phone on the wooden dresser and sat on the edge of her bed.

Amanda gazed across the room and found her reflection on the mirror of her dresser. She looked at herself to find that her complexion was everything but composed. Her long hair was slightly disheveled and her face was whiter than usual. Her eyes followed down the thin dark streaks that mixed into her long, blonde hair.

Darkness...

Amanda thought back to the day when she had awakened to discover her new appearance in the bathroom mirror. The darkness had begun to physically show how it was beginning to affect her.

Going back to her roots, she had been born blonde and raised by her angelic grandmother.

The blonde was light and she had been raised by the Light.

Balance could be a good thing.

In the end, she had a mix of both, proving to show that even her hair was a combination of two completely different colors. Representing the two worlds of which she had been created.

Space... space might be a good thing to get the balance that she needed...

It was silent when the phone abruptly began to buzz. It created a loud, obnoxious sound between the wood and the plastic as the phone slowly danced across the top of her dresser.

Amanda closed her eyes tightly, as she tried to resist the urge to pick up her cell phone.

The sound of the vibrating phone seemed to grow louder and louder, as if it were yelling at her to answer its call.

The phone had crawled to the edge of the dresser and tipped over the side. Amanda anticipated the sound of it falling to the floor but it never happened.

A breeze swept into the room and she opened her eyes to find that Mitch had caught the phone before it even had a chance to hit the wooden planks.

Unaware that she had been holding her breath, she opened her eyes to find Mitch standing before her.

She exhaled quietly and tried to compose herself without him noticing anything too unusual or out of the ordinary.

The moment had been surprisingly intense and typically when she saw Mitch, everything seemed to come together and feel as if everything were in their proper place. But seeing him didn't make her feel as relieved as she thought it would.

Amanda loved him and she always would, but she was starting to realize that a line had to be drawn in order to keep a balance. She could only hope that he would understand that she was doing it not only for herself but for the both of them.

Mitch carefully placed the phone back onto the dresser and walked over to Amanda.

It was obvious.

She couldn't hide her feelings from him. She was never good at it. Of all the things she'd mastered, concealing her emotions was something she could never perfect.

Mitch could sense that something wasn't right and Amanda anticipated his first question.

"Why didn't you pick up your phone?" Mitch asked.

Just what she expected.

Amanda's stomach slowly sank simultaneously with the depression of the bed as he sat down beside her. Her first instinct was to lean into his warm embrace but she couldn't bring herself to do it. Amanda refused to give in to what her heart yearned for and decided to remain adamant.

What should she say? How could she explain what she wanted to do or what was on her mind?

They could talk about anything, right? Why was it suddenly so difficult?

Her head started to hurt once again as she felt the complexity of the two different emotions. The feeling was all too familiar and she hated it.

Luca had to be right. Too much darkness was not a good thing, but why were his words having such a strong influence on her way of thinking all of a sudden?

It was her better judgment and it was no longer dormant like it had been for so long. It was alive within her and she needed to make it known.

Her heart wanted one thing but her mind told her something different. Luca had opened up her mind into actually considering that maybe she really was being irrational after all. Darkness was overwhelmingly consuming her heart and she needed a balance in order to learn how to live in order to prevent these painful dueling emotions within her.

It was the only way and she could only hope that he would understand.

"I… I was going to call you back. I just wanted to have some time to myself first." Amanda fumbled her words before she continued. "It was a long day."

Amanda had never been at a loss for words or lost such confidence in herself before. Amanda couldn't even look at him without feeling like she was being forced to do something she didn't really want to do.

It's okay... just talk.

Mitch's snicker caught her off guard.

"I bet it was a long day after meeting that new Watcher. Was he as annoying as Gregg? I really do hate those... creatures." Mitch winced. "I know Gregg's your friend but I don't know how you could stand to be around him sometimes. I can't."

"Well... I know. But it wasn't that bad and this guy was a little more laid back. His name is Luca and he's... nice."

"Well, if he's so nice, then what's going on? You seem like you're a little down or something. I can sense it. Are you alright?" Mitch asked as he leaned in, attempting to look her in the eyes but she refrained.

The Demon lifted his hand to her chin and gently brushed her skin, guiding her eyes to meet his.

Irresistible... why did he have to be so seductive, so ridiculously alluring?

Once she saw the dark eyes she had grown to love so dearly, it felt as if the difficulty bar had been raised to the very top and her breathe caught in her throat.

How could she tell him that space might be a good thing for them?

Mitch could tell that she was struggling to say something. He placed his hand on hers in an attempt to reassure her that he was there for her and willing to listen.

"I'm fine." Amanda said finally.

Mitch's eyes narrowed in, gazing right at her, as if he could see into her soul.

"Now, I know you better than that. You can tell me. I know something's going on and you're too stubborn to tell me what it is. Sometimes you can be the worst liar." Mitch said, smiling at her. "And we both know that's something you need to work on."

His face was so close to hers that his body heat warmed her cheeks causing them to blush a light pink.

Tell him what you're thinking... why are you being so damn stubborn?

"I..."

The words just wouldn't come.

Mitch leaned in and kissed her gently as his warm hand caressed the nape of her neck. She gave in and felt the butterflies flutter within her stomach at the soft touch of his lips pressing onto hers.

Each and every moment they shared a kiss, it felt as though it could last forever. She inhaled the familiar sweet yet spicy scent of firewood that she always found so incredibly enticing. He always managed to take her breath away with one kiss or one simple touch and it never got old.

He slowly pulled away as his hand slid down her side and onto her thigh. Mitch patiently waited for her response, locking his eyes once again with hers.

Amanda tried to fight against what her heart so passionately ached for. It was the most difficult thing that anyone could ever endure. Love was always worth fighting for, but in order to love, sometimes sacrifices were essential to making it work.

Amanda's stomach churned because she knew that he wouldn't take well to hearing that a Watcher had given her the advice. The last thing she wanted was to be away from him again, but it was for the better, it was to ensure that in the end they could be together.

But... would he understand?

The only way to find out was to tell him the truth about what she reluctantly knew what she had to do. Amanda knew that it was going to be arduous but to figure out what the heart wants versus what the mind dictates, it would never be easy to fathom.

She had to make this choice. But would he understand that the space would be temporary?

All she wanted was to create a balance in order to ensure that they could be together without any sort of greater influence from the light or the darkness.

Here we go...

"Space."

The word slipped breathlessly out of her mouth before she even realized she had said anything.

"What?" Mitch asked curiously with a look of confusion.

Amanda took a deep breath and looked away before she spoke again.

"I think we need some... space." She repeated.

"What? Why?" Mitch asked, looking confused.

Amanda could hear the tone in his voice drop and she automatically knew that he wasn't going to understand.

This wasn't going to be easy...

It felt as if she were suddenly a million miles away from him, so distant it made her stomach crumble into nothing but the truth needed to come out.

Just do it. Just say it.

"I need a balance. I need a break from darkness. I feel like I need to work with my White Light. I just feel unbalanced and it's been too long. I've been feeling a little overwhelmed and I need... space. Just for a little while." Amanda said, and waited for his reaction.

Mitch was quiet for a moment before he clenched his fists and he started bursting at the seams with anger.

"Space? Damn it, Amanda. It's Gregg, isn't it? Gregg told you to do this!" The Demon said through his tightly gritted teeth.

Amanda could sense his anger building and she immediately regretted saying anything at all.

She didn't want him to be angry. She just needed him to understand.

"Don't you understand that he's trying to pull you away from me?" Mitch asked as he stood up and walked away from her.

"Don't walk away from me! It's not Gregg! This is *my* decision and I'm doing it because I know that I need a balance. I'm not going to get anywhere if I only practice one side of me. I need to know how to work my Light too. I need to learn both in order to live and make *us* work. I can't deal with these headaches anymore." Amanda tried to be as honest as she could.

"But you learned how to control your headaches, you just need to concentrate." Mitch said.

"No, you don't understand. It's been getting worse and worse and I can't control them as much as I could before. I need to do this, just please, understand." Amanda pleaded.

"I know Gregg has something to do with this and he's trying to pull you away from me! How do you expect me to understand when you don't want to be with me?" Mitch yelled with his back to her.

"It's not Gregg! Stop saying that because I can think for myself! Luca…"

"Luca?!" Mitch interrupted and turned around with a surprised look on his face. "This new Watcher is trying to make you change your mind about being with me?!"

"No! Please, Mitch! He only made me think twice about what I was doing, but he *never* told me to stay away from you. Mitch, you know that I love you but I really think that space will be good for us in order for me to learn more about the White Light I have inside me. I need to form a balance so things like this won't happen in the future. Please, it's not what you're making it out to be!" Amanda said, desperately begging him to be reasonable.

"Look at us, Amanda. The past two months have been working out fine and nothing has happened! And if something *were* to happen, I need to be here to protect you. Remember what happened the last time you wanted space?"

"I know what happened but this is different now. I have to do this, and it's not just for me, it's for us and if you can't even try to understand that, then I..." Amanda didn't know where she was taking the conversation but if he couldn't understand, then so be it. "...I think you should leave."

Mitch's hands dropped to his sides in defeat. He couldn't believe what he was hearing.

"I can't believe we're going through this again after what happened before! But fine, have it your way. If you want me gone, then I'm gone. This is your choice, not mine." Mitch said angrily and stomped his foot.

"Stop being so childish and try to understand!" Amanda said. "I knew this was going to happen! Why can't you just listen to what I'm saying and stop making it all about you?"

The memory of her argument with Nan surfaced into her mind when the words came out of her mouth. Amanda recalled her grandmother saying the same exact thing to her when Nan was simply trying to explain the reasoning and advice she had been trying to give her. It dawned on her that the darkness was truly having an immense pull on her and had been influencing her the entire time she'd been with Mitch.

"I want to protect you and I want to be with you but you're letting these Watchers dictate your life!" Mitch yelled back at her.

Amanda could feel the tension in the room as if it were a cloud of smoke making it increasingly harder for her to breathe.

"Are you serious? No one is telling me what to do! Didn't we go through this? How many times do I have to tell you that I need to do this for us and it's my *own* decision!"

Amanda found herself actually yelling at him and she couldn't contain herself. She wasn't going to be judged any longer and she desperately needed for him to understand her point of view.

"Who knows what could happen when I barely know how to use my White Light? What if we needed it in order to protect myself, or even to protect you?"

"I can protect myself! I don't need anyone else!" Mitch retorted nastily.

"I can't believe you right now! Just because you're a Demon doesn't mean you're strong enough to fight off anything that comes your way! We learned that last time, didn't we? And you didn't save me, Nan did!" Amanda yelled back.

The words were like a slap to his face and she could see it deep in his eyes. Mitch was a stone wall and he wasn't going to see it any other way, especially after what she had just said. But he had to hear the truth and how else was she going to explain or get through to him?

If he couldn't understand and he refused to listen, then what else was there to say?

She could feel the lump forming in the back of her throat and tears were building up from behind her eyes.

Amanda never wanted this to happen.

Not like this.

He was a Demon after all so how could she expect him to completely understand all the time?

"Fine, have it your way." Mitch said after a few moments of silence.

Mitch swiftly walked over to the open bedroom window in an attempt to leave.

"Please…" Amanda said.

Mitch stopped with his back to her but he was too stubborn to respond.

"Please, still come with me to prom on Saturday? I can't let Alexia down and I promised her that we'd go, remember? We'll get past this. Just try to understand. I need you in my life. I can't lose you. We have an immortal love, remember?"

Mitch turned his head slightly to acknowledge what she had said but remained silent.

"Please, just, say something." Amanda pleaded.

Amanda felt so cold and alone with only his back toward her. She crossed her arms on her chest in an attempt to hold and comfort herself if he wasn't going to. She watched him with glazed eyes as he stood there, motionless and facing the open window away from her.

Amanda felt the tears tumble down her cheeks and in the blink of an eye, he was gone.

Chapter 6

RESTLESS

The next morning, Amanda tried to focus on the white board at the front of the classroom. The school day was almost over but her vision was still hazy and her mind cloudy after an entire night without sleep.

The night had felt like it went on forever and her body felt weak and exhausted from tossing and turning, crying and sobbing. She missed Mitch and wished he would have simply understood what she was trying to do, what she was trying to explain. It was not just for herself but for them both.

He was her world and the last thing she wanted was to be away from him once again. But she knew it was the right thing to do in order to focus on her other side without any distractions. She had needs and he couldn't understand that?

Regret...

Should she have said anything at all? Could she have gotten around it without forcing him out temporarily once again?

Amanda knew that she hadn't done anything wrong, but she regretted what she had said to Mitch. The words echoed in her mind and the look in his eyes expressed nothing else but hurt.

"Just because you're a Demon doesn't mean you're strong enough to fight off anything that comes your way and we learned that last time, didn't we? You didn't save me, Nan did!"

Amanda sighed and held her head in her hands.

Was there never an easy way out? How could she expect that dating a Demon was going to be that simple?

The image of his back to her made her feel so cold and forlorn. He hadn't even spoken a word to her before he vanished. The only hope Amanda was dwelling on was that it was one fight that they could get past. It was a misunderstanding that they had to deal with and everything would end up being alright in the end.

Right?

The bell rang and Amanda was the last to get up out of her chair and exit the classroom.

As she held her notebook and walked down the hallway, she could feel her wings drooping lifelessly behind her, dragging on the tiled floor.

Amanda turned the corner to find Alexia at her locker like usual.

"What's wrong?" Alexia asked, noticing Amanda's saddened expression.

Amanda opened her locker and placed her notebook in between her other textbooks without saying a word. Alexia waited for Amanda to respond but it never came.

"Oh, this is bad. I can tell." Alexia said and leaned into the other locker beside Amanda's. "What happened?"

Amanda shut the locker door and hesitated before looking her best friend eye to eye.

"We…" Amanda paused. "We had a fight. I made a choice he didn't like and I thought he would understand, but he didn't. I should've known better. But I don't even know what I was expecting to come out of it any way."

"Ok, we need to talk about this. Listen, let's have a girl's night. I'll come over after dinner and we'll talk about it! Tomorrow we have to go prom dress shopping any way so we can talk about that too."

Amanda knew Alexia was trying to help and for the first time in a while, she wanted more than anything to talk with her closest friend.

"Okay, I'll see you later after dinner." Amanda said, trying to hold back her tears. It felt so good to have a friend to share everything with and despite the argument they had before, it was as if it never happened.

Amanda wanted more than anything to have a girl's night with Alexia. Maybe getting her mind off Mitch for one night would be a good thing.

———*ozoz*———

"So, he just… left?" Alexia asked, dumbfounded.

"Yep, just vanished right there without saying anything at

all." Amanda sadly confirmed and gestured to her window.

"Wow." Alexia said with disbelief. She was sprawled out on her stomach across Amanda's bed, flipping through a magazine while Amanda sat on the floor, reluctant to pick up a single magazine of the many that cluttered the floor.

"Didn't he hear anything you were telling him? I know he cares about you, I mean, he acts like he would even like take a bullet for you, or I guess take a hit of White Light for you but I'm shocked he would just leave you like that and not listen to what you have to say."

"I guess I can't expect a Demon to do the right thing, or at least not all the time." Amanda explained. "It's just, I want to do the right thing for the both of us. It'll make it easier in the future, you know? I care about him so much but when Luca said what he did the other day, it made me think about what's best for me and what I need, not necessarily what I want, which is Mitch, obviously."

"Luca does have a point. I think you're doing the right thing. I think space is good, even if Mitch doesn't get it." Alexia said, agreeing with her friend and putting the magazine down at her side.

"There's one thing I regret though." Amanda said reluctantly.

"What?" Alexia asked as she sat up and leaned forward.

"I kind of said something that really hurt him." Amanda said, recalling the memory. "I was getting fed up with him telling me that I wasn't thinking for myself. So, in a way, I kind of threw in his face that just because he is who he is, doesn't mean he's the strongest thing around. I kind of, in other words, said that he didn't save my life, Nan did and he's not as strong as he thinks he is."

Alexia looked back at Amanda with a surprised expression.

"You said that?" Alexia asked.

"Yeah, but I shouldn't have. He did everything he could to try and save me even though he couldn't. I was just so angry that I threw it in his face. You saw everything that happened at Sea Grove that night and there really wasn't much he could do when Nan came into the picture. I just know that I hurt him when I said that, and I didn't mean to."

"I'm actually kind of impressed that you told him straight up how it was. Don't be so hard on yourself because he had to calm down with the cocky attitude of his at some point and if he wasn't even going to listen to what you had to say, why not give it to him straight? He's got to hear it from someone and who else better to do that than you?" Alexia said and shrugged.

"I guess, but I hope he forgives me. I just don't even know if Demons can even forgive. I mean last time I was the one who forgave him but this is different this time. We've been through a lot in the past two months and he's taught me more ways in dealing with my darker side. He's been there for me and we've been together so much."

"You don't have to tell me twice." Alexia huffed.

"I know, but I'm working on it now. I know I can't spend all of my time with him. I need a balance and it's tougher to do than it sounds." Amanda tried to explain.

"I know, it's fine. You don't have to justify it for me. I get it, and you know I do." Alexia said and smiled.

"I just hope he loves me enough to forgive me and we can get past this. He brought up that the last time I wanted space, something bad happened. I just hope he's not right and something bad happens this time too."

"I doubt it, I mean I know it's been quiet, or too quiet like Gregg says but what could a little space do? You got to do what you got to do if you want to get your head straight. And if he doesn't get it, then he doesn't get it." Alexia shrugged again.

"True, I guess."

Amanda glanced down at a magazine in front of her on the floor that displayed a male model in a suit standing next to a girl in a prom dress on the cover.

"Mitch's supposed to go with Gregg to get his tux. Do you know if Gregg's heard from Mitch at all today?" Amanda asked, hoping that Alexia would say yes.

"I don't think so, but Gregg hasn't told me any different so I'm sure everything will be fine. Don't get too worked up about it, I mean, I know that Mitch is crazy about you. There's no way that you guys are over or anything." Alexia said as she tossed her legs over the end of the bed.

The thought of ending their relationship made her gut queasy and that was the last thing she wanted. All she could do was hope that he would eventually forgive her when the time was right. Everything would get better within a few days and in time for prom.

Right?

"Okay, enough of the drama." Alexia said in an attempt to change the subject as she reached down and grabbed a handful of magazines from off the floor. "You guys will be fine and dandy and before you know it, prom will be here! It's going to be fun, I promise! Everything will be fine in the end, so don't worry too much! It's weird because usually you're the one who tells me not to worry."

"Okay." Amanda said quietly. Her friend had a good point and all she could do is hope for the best for the time being.

"Now, pick up a magazine and start going through these dresses! Tomorrow after school, we are going shopping!" Alexia said excitedly. "I was thinking we could go out to West Branch Mall."

"We haven't been there in a while." Amanda said sadly, her attitude unchanged.

"Right? It's about a half hour drive but I figure, what the hell? We haven't been there in a long time and there are a lot of dress stores to look at!"

"True."

Alexia plopped her hands down onto her thighs with a loud slap.

"Come on, Amanda, at least cheer up a little bit." Alexia said, frustrated with Amanda's lack of excitement.

"I will, I will." Amanda said and looked up at Alexia with a weak smile. "I'm sorry, I'll try. I promise."

"Okay fine." Alexia smiled and dove back into the magazine. "Any way, what color do you think you want to go with? I was thinking maybe pink for myself, or maybe even blue. Well, actually this purple color isn't bad either."

Amanda glanced down at the floor around her, and picked up one of the magazines, and started flipping through the pages.

"Wait a minute, do that thing again! I just want to make sure we're set for tomorrow!" Alexia said, encouraging Amanda to work her magic.

Amanda reached into her pocket and conjured up the desire for what she needed. She closed her eyes and concentrated carefully.

After a moment, she pulled out two fifty dollars bills and displayed them on the palm of her hand.

"Awesome! That is so cool! We are definitely going all out tomorrow!" Alexia said. "You know, you still have to show me how you glow and stuff! You've been spending so much time with Mitch that we haven't even gotten there yet!"

Amanda chuckled as Alexia regained her focus back on her magazine.

Amanda decided that she was going to try and get through the night without thinking about Mitch. After all, she was the one who wanted space so she could focus on her light and take a break from the overpowering hold of darkness.

The night was about spending time with Alexia and trying to figure out what to plan for what Alexia considered the most important event of senior year, the Senior Prom.

Chapter 7

FACING THE TRUTH

After Alexia left for the night, Amanda brushed her teeth and changed into her pajama shorts and a tee-shirt. As she got ready to go to sleep for the night, Oreo had wondered into her room and waited for her on the bed.

All she could do was try to stay positive but it was so difficult to comprehend. She knew that Mitch was upset with her and that was the last thing she had wanted to happen.

What else could she expect from a Demon? But he was stronger and better than that, right?

Had she been wrong?

She refused to believe that she was wrong about him. She loved him and surprisingly enough, had faith in him. He had seen the light in her when they first met. He had even said she had proved to him that there was so much more than the darkness.

But could the darkness had been growing stronger within him just as much as it was affecting her when they were together?

It had to be true because he was acting completely different and he wasn't being as understanding as he had been in the beginning.

After she switched off her desk lamp, she walked over to her window and slid it open. Despite the little hope she had that Mitch would sneak into her room like he had made a habit of doing, she left it open just to make herself feel a little better.

Amanda glanced outside and through the branches of the tree outside. The night sky was a dark navy blue and the moon hung high as it spilled the bright moonlight into her room.

The vision of Mitch sitting alone in their open field just outside of town was a vivid image in her mind. In her heart, all she wanted was to be lying next to him in the long grass, looking up at the stars like they did on so many nights.

Space… space is the best thing right now…

Amanda crawled into bed as Oreo snuggled up close to her, offering the slightest bit of comfort. Amanda smiled and nuzzled up to her puppy, reciprocating and welcoming the offered affection.

After a few silent moments, Amanda was just about to close her eyes and drift off when a barely audible sound knocked on her bedroom door.

"Amanda?" Nan asked through the door.

"Yes?"

"Can I come in?"

Considering the unenthusiastic mood Amanda was in, she took in a deep breath and exhaled before granting her grandmother's request to enter. She really wasn't in the mood to talk and all she wanted was to fall asleep and welcome the dream world to escape from reality.

Dreams hadn't come to visit her in a while but considering how she was feeling, she'd even appreciate a nightmare just to take her away from the unwanted situation she had put herself in.

Something... anything else but this...

"Yep." Amanda simply replied and turned over on her side to face the door.

The door opened slowly and Nan walked into the room.

"Can we talk?" Nan asked.

"About what?" Amanda asked, slightly annoyed.

"Well, I know you're going through a tough time and I'm not just here to try and guide you but I'm here for you to talk to. Like we used to, remember?" Nan said and gingerly sat down beside Amanda on her small bed. "I want to remind you that I'm not just your grandmother, I'm your friend too."

Amanda didn't know what to say. The last time she and her grandmother spoke hadn't ended well.

"Despite our significant differences, I want you to understand that I will always forgive you." Nan explained.

When Amanda looked up at her grandmother, she felt herself calm down and relax more than she expected. She already had been away from Mitch for a little more than a day and she could feel the change in her energy.

Nan looked down at her granddaughter and waited patiently for her response. The moon's light created a glow around Nan and it reminded Amanda of the first time when her grandmother revealed her true form, as a Sebalim Angel.

The woman had appeared so beautiful, so serene, so angelic. She recalled the heavenly voice of her grandmother and she could only imagine what the Kingdom of Heaven's chorus of Angel's music sounded like. Amanda was amazed when she saw that side of her grandmother and it made her yearn to know more. But she became so consumed with darkness and being with Mitch that she had almost forgotten what it was like.

The thought made her reminisce about the night when Gregg had taken her to her high school's football field. She had begun to learn how to bring forth the light right through and out of her entire body.

In truth, as she continued to think about it, she genuinely missed how it felt. The coolness running beneath her skin felt extraordinary and the ability to fly was simply indescribable.

It was time to get back to it... further explore her light.

The first thing she had to do was apologize to Nan after the things she had said and the way she had acted. The one person who had raised her, cared for her and always been there for her didn't deserve to be treated the way she had.

"I know, Nan." Amanda finally said. "I'm... sorry for what I said the other day. I've been thinking and I know I've been spending too much time with Mitch."

"Oh, young love." Nan smiled and laughed to herself. "I understand, darling. It's one of the most difficult wonders of life, love. It's a blessing and a curse, like yourself. It's hard to keep up with and maintain, unless you form a balance."

Nan always knew the right things to say and she was never far off from the truth.

Amanda sat up quickly and looked her grandmother directly in her eyes.

"That's exactly what I'm trying to do. But it's so hard! I love him so much, but it gets kind of overwhelming at times. I mean I know he's a Demon and you don't necessarily approve but he *has* helped me. He's taught me things I need about my dark powers but I'm also starting to understand that I need to know the other side too! He just... doesn't understand, I guess." Amanda said as she shifted her gaze toward her window.

"Nothing is easy, Amanda. Challenges are what make us grow. They are what make us stronger and more willing to learn. And you are facing many challenges right now. And I know not having your parents here is probably making it all the more complicated for you." Nan said, placing her hand on Amanda's.

"Tell me about it…" Amanda said sarcastically about the tender topic. "Why haven't they shown up? When will I see them? Will I ever see them?"

"Well, your father disappeared long ago. He is a Demon after all and I can't speak for him. But I'm sure your mother will arrive when the proper moment comes. I'm sure that they would be here for you when they feel a need to intervene." Nan tried to explain.

"But isn't right *now* a *proper moment*? I mean now that everyone knows what I really am, shouldn't she step into the picture? The least she could do is be here for me." Amanda said.

"Your mother is a bright and beautiful Angel. They will make their decisions when they need to. There's a reason for everything and I'm sure she'd be here if she deemed that now was appropriate, Amanda. They love you. I know it's hard to comprehend that they are not here right now, but they will be in due time. And I'm sure she's been hearing the prayers you've been sending."

"How do you know about that?" Amanda asked, taken by surprise.

Nan raised her eyebrows, giving Amanda an allusive glance.

"I know, I know. Okay, I think I knew the answer to that one but I didn't think *you* were listening. I just thought maybe I can get her to hear me or maybe even come to me."

"I think it's wonderful that you have been practicing your praying. It's a way of communication that I'm sure you'll find useful in the future. Remember when Gregg said a prayer for you and I was able to make it in time to save you from that terrifying fall?" Nan said and cringed at the horrifying memory.

"Yea, it's kind of hard to forget." Amanda said

"For reasons like those, that is why prayer is so very important. But don't lose faith in your mother because there is a reason for everything. I'm sure she is doing the right thing even if you don't agree. The time will come. You just need to be patient and let things take their course."

Amanda sighed and leaned back into her pillow, staring up at the ceiling. She knew her grandmother was right, she always was but the anxiety was killing her.

"I just want answers! I feel so... lost." Amanda said helplessly.

She hadn't confided in her grandmother in what seemed like forever and it felt so relieving to just say what was going through her mind. However, she just had to take her grandmother's advice and accept things as they were. Amanda had almost forgotten how wise and helpful her grandmother truly was.

"You are not lost, my dear. Even though your fate is still uncertain, stay true to your faith and in due time, everything will be laid out before you. Strength is all you need and strength is what you have. I believe in you." Nan said with a warm grin. "Everyone has one life in which to determine their destiny and yours is one very special life."

Amanda smiled and rolled onto her side, facing away from her grandmother.

"Nan?"

"Yes? What is it, angel?" Nan asked.

"Can you sing me to sleep?"

"Of course I will. Remember when I used to do that when you were little?" Nan asked, beaming as she recalled the memory.

Amanda nodded her head and smiled at the fond and loving memory. She nestled up with her puppy and rested her chin gently on Oreo's little head.

The sound of the elderly woman's voice floated into the air as she sang a harmonious tune.

The image of the little innocent girl from years ago that hadn't a clue about her future emerged from her memories. The little girl she used to be, the one who hadn't yet discovered what was hidden behind everything she thought she knew.

Everything she believed in.

Going way back before she knew her grandmother's singing had a whole other meaning.

The soothing melody was stunningly beautiful and sweet and within minutes, Amanda had drifted off into a deep and peaceful sleep.

Chapter 8

QUALITY TIME

"Put the cell phone away and forget about him for just today, alright? This is about prom and not boyfriend drama right now." Alexia said as she glanced over at Amanda from behind the steering wheel of her Audi.

The cell phone was sitting in the palm of her hand and Amanda couldn't help but feel the constant urge to text or call Mitch. She wanted to say sorry but he was just too stubborn to understand.

What more could she expect from a Demon, but he was different, wasn't he?

Regardless, she missed him desperately.

"But what if he doesn't meet with Gregg to pick out his tux? What if he doesn't come with me to prom? What if he just..."

"Stop with the *what ifs*. If he goes with Gregg, he goes. I highly doubt he would just ditch you. We've gone through this Amanda.

He's crazy about you, I can see it when he looks at you. You had a fight, they happen. God knows, I understand that part after fighting with Gregg over finding everything out, remember? Besides, you're the one who wanted space, right?" Alexia asked.

Amanda hesitated before nodding her head.

She was right.

"Yeah..."

"Okay, well he's giving it to you, like you asked. I know you said it'd didn't go over well and I know that it's probably hard but today's not about that. It's supposed to be fun, so let's just shop and get your mind off of it, okay?"

Amanda knew better than to dwell on it, but she couldn't help herself. Their argument hadn't even ended on a good note and that didn't help things either.

"Fine. I'm sorry." Amanda said and put her phone on vibrate. She reluctantly slipped her phone into the pocket of her jean shorts and took a deep breath. She tried to push her thoughts of Mitch aside and told herself to focus on her day with Alexia. "You're right, let's just have fun."

"That's more like it!" Alexia said excitedly. "And who knows, maybe we'll find the most amazing dress that will make him come crawling back to you, apologizing for being such a jerk!"

"Yeah, that'd be nice." Amanda said with a slight smile on her face but rolling her eyes.

Like that would ever happen.

After finally turning off the main highway, they pulled into the expansive parking lot of West Branch Mall to find it quite crowded. It was a two story shopping center with over one hundred and fifty stores and restaurants. If a girl wanted a full day of shopping, this would be the place to get it done.

Alexia managed to find a close parking space and pulled in as fast as she could before anyone else could take it.

By the time they had gotten there, it was four o'clock, leaving them plenty of time to shop before closing at nine that night.

"Are you ready to find the dress of your dreams?!" Alexia asked as she grabbed the handle of her car door, more than ready to jump out and probably sprint to the front entrance.

Amanda marveled at Alexia's enthusiasm and her ability to lighten the mood over something she found so exciting.

"Ready as I'll ever be!" Amanda replied cheerfully and opened the car door.

She got out of the car to find the exterior of the mall had been updated with a new look. The mall was now colored a tan shade and the front entrance had tall white columns and plants lining the walls.

It might have appeared a little too extravagant and it left Amanda wondering what the interior had altered to be.

When it came down to the town of West Branch, everything was high end and more expensive, given its location and general population. The houses were huge and mansions overwhelming. The wealthy and well off people lived in the town and its reputation was very well known.

The last time they had been there was the beginning of the school year when Alexia insisted that they get new clothes to start off senior year.

It wasn't often that they'd go there but Alexia insisted on going to West Branch Mall, given that Amanda could make any amount of money appear in her hand.

They could buy anything they wanted and not feel guilty about it.

With Alexia's fashion advice, and unlimited money, there was no doubt that they wouldn't be able to find their dream dresses in West Branch Mall.

Chapter 9

BLUR

"*A*manda! Come look at this one!" Alexia called across the department store.

Amanda hung up the pale green dress she had been admiring and turned away, in search of Alexia.

Phillip's was one of the largest and most popular department stores known for their high end commodities. From clothes to furniture and jewelry to perfumes, the store had everything to offer.

From the moment they had entered the store, they had both wondered off in different directions. Amanda found herself more interested in the solid and simple cocktail dresses while Alexia had bolted over to the section that contained the sparkly, form fitting and brightly colored ball gowns.

"Where are you?" Amanda called out above the many clothing racks.

"Over here!"

Amanda walked in the direction of her friend's voice as she glanced around, observing the many colored dresses throughout the large store.

She rounded the corner to find Alexia holing up an extravagant purple ball gown up against the front her body. It looked as if it weighed a ton with all the jewels on the bodice but Alexia didn't seem to struggle with it. When it came to fashion, it didn't matter how heavy or grand it was. Alexia would make it work if she truly loved it.

"What do you think of this one? Isn't it amazing?" Alexia asked, beaming with a big smile.

It was too busy and big for Amanda's taste but if she knew Alexia well enough, Alexia would come across something she'd love even more. Sometimes it was impossible to get Alexia to finally reach the register without changing her mind a hundred times.

Just before Amanda could voice her opinion, Alexia's eyes widened quickly as she looked past Amanda.

Three... Two... One...

"What a minute! What about that one?" Alexia rushed past Amanda and grabbed a different dress as she hung the purple one back up on another rack.

"I think I like this one better! I think blue would look great with my hair, what do you think?" Alexia asked.

Amanda held her breath for a moment and when she realized her friend was going to let her talk this time, she decided to finally talk.

"I like that one! It's really pretty and the light blue would definitely work!" Amanda said as she watched her friend glow as she inspected the dress thoroughly.

"Oh my God, it has a corset in the back too! I have to try this on!" Alexia said and turned as if she were ready to sprint down the store isle to the dressing room. "Wait."

Alexia turned back around to face Amanda. "Did you find a dress?"

"I saw one over there but I'm still not sure." Amanda said, pointing across the store.

"We'll find you something, don't worry!" Alexia said and grabbed Amanda's hand. "But come with me and I'll try this on. I think this might be the one!"

Amanda wasn't in the least bit worried about not finding a dress. In fact, if she had it her way, she wouldn't even go to prom but she was obligated to and she had to keep reminding herself that.

Alexia dragged Amanda to the dressing room and Amanda sat on a small stool, waiting patiently for Alexia to come out and flaunt around in the dress.

"So, what color do you think you want to go with?" Alexia asked through the dressing room door.

"I was thinking maybe... green." Amanda said, glancing around the dressing room. There was a row of singular dressing cubicles and three elongated mirrors side by side in the corner.

Amanda leaned back against the wall as her hands plopped down onto her thighs. She could feel her phone inside her pocket beneath her palm. It was difficult to resist the urge of sliding it out with the hopes of Mitch contacting her. But she knew he hadn't, because she never felt it vibrate.

"Green? Well, what kind of green?" Alexia asked, as her voice strained and Amanda could only assume that she was trying to slide into the bodice of the dress.

"I'm not sure, maybe..." Amanda's breath caught in her throat and her stomach dropped. She did a double take as her glance crossed past the mirrors.

She could have sworn that she saw something. Something she'd never seen before, but it was so fast, she couldn't even make out what she had seen. Whatever it was, it was gone in the blink of an eye.

It was something dark. Possibly something resembling a shadow; a tall, black blur.

What was it? Was it her imagination?

Amanda felt as if something was off and she knew it couldn't have been her imagination.

Suddenly, her senses were acutely aware of everything in the room, but nothing was there. There was nothing to be found other than she, Alexia, the mirrors and a rack of mismatched clothes.

She stood up and wondered over to the mirrors to get a better look, but all she saw was her reflection starring back at her.

"Amanda? What's wrong?" Alexia asked.

Amanda reached out to touch the mirror when she noticed Alexia in the reflection behind her.

"Nothing, nothing's wrong." Amanda turned around and saw her friend in the grand ball, sky blue ball gown.

"Can you help me with the corset?" Alexia asked as she turned around and lifted her hair up past her shoulders.

"Sure." Amanda smiled and took hold of the blue ribbons.

After she pulled and pushed for a few moments, Amanda finally tied the ribbons into a beautiful big bow and they both turned to face the mirror.

Alexia was glowing and the look on her face said it all.

It was the ideal choice.

The blue gown was strapless and had a sweet heart shaped lining on the top. The lustrous satin tightly hugged around her body in layers with blue and silver beading that glistened in the proper lighting. The dress came out at the waist and sprawled out around her, reach down to the floor.

"You look amazing!" Amanda said, admiring how beautiful the dress fit Alexia.

"This is it! It's amazing! Wait until everyone sees!" Alexia said, bouncing on the tips of her toes. "I don't even want to take it off! But now we have to find you a dress!"

They both smiled and Alexia turned and hurriedly ran back into the dressing room to quickly change.

Amanda walked cautiously over to the mirror one last time before Alexia could pop out of the dressing room.

What did she see?

Chapter 10

RUBY RED

After a couple hours of visiting store after store, Amanda couldn't seem to find a dress that she wanted. Nothing seemed to stand out and it was getting late. The mall was set to close soon and she had tried on a multitude of various dresses.

Alexia insisted she broaden her horizons and get something different, something she wouldn't ordinarily buy.

Alexia made her try on dresses from pink to purple to yellow and teal but all of them either didn't look right or fit on her awkwardly.

"This is harder than I thought." Alexia said as they both walked out of yet another store, empty handed.

"I'm sorry, but I'm just not crazy about any of the ones we looked at and some of them just didn't fit right. Maybe we should go somewhere else instead? Maybe one of the shops in Middleton?"

"Are you kidding me? We won't find anything there and besides, if we're going to find anything at all, it's got to be here. Trust me." Alexia said as she continued on, hauling the blue gown in the big dress bag and her purse over her shoulder.

Alexia glanced in each store window, constantly looking to see if there were any dress stores they might have missed.

Amanda sighed and kept walking along side Alexia with two plastic bags of prom accessories. They were able to find Alexia shoes and even jewelry to match her dress but Amanda couldn't find *the one.*

A dress.

"Wait! What about that store? Did we go there?" Alexia pointed across the way, next to a puppy store.

"I don't think so, but we could go to the puppy store." Amanda said.

"Well, it figures that you'd be more interested in puppies than dresses." Alexia rolled her eyes and followed Amanda toward the puppy shop.

Amanda peered through the glass and tapped her finger on the window, trying to interact with the little Pug puppy that was romping around in the pen.

"He's so cute! Look at him! Sometimes I just want to get another dog for Oreo to play with. He needs a buddy. Oh! And that one over there looks just like Oreo!" Amanda said pointing to the dogs.

"Maybe *Oreo* needs a buddy, but I know what you need. You need a dress! Come on, let's go into this place. We didn't look in here yet." Alexia said grabbing Amanda's arm and pulling her away from the puppy in the window.

Amanda grudgingly went along with Alexia into the shop next door. The shop sign read Allure Fashion Boutique in bright orange and cursive letters.

"This place is... nice!" Alexia said as they entered the store.

The entire store consisted of various formal styles from women's dresses to men's suits.

"Welcome to Allure, ladies! My name is Lily, what can I help you with today?"

A slender, young woman with blonde hair, dressed in a black mini dress had walked out from the back door of the shop. She swiftly walked toward the front of the store as she welcomed Amanda and Alexia into the boutique.

"Hi! We need help finding a prom dress for my friend!" Alexia said, gesturing to Amanda. "We've been everywhere and we can't find the right dress for her."

"Prom? How exciting!" The woman said clapping her hands together.

Amanda sifted through the gold dress rack closest to her when some movement across the store caught her eye. She peered above the rack to find a tall bald man behind the register, counting money.

"Amanda! Answer the lady! I can't answer for you because anything I pick out hasn't been working." Alexia said.

"Sorry, I... umm... what did you say?" Amanda asked, turning her gaze to the saleswoman.

"I wanted to know what kind of dress you were looking for?" The saleswoman raised her eye brows, waiting patiently for her response.

"I guess I'm looking for something not so big, not so sparkly either. Just kind of basic." Amanda said.

"We have just the thing for you! And please, ladies, call me Lily! Follow me this way."

Amanda and Alexia followed the woman toward the back of the store where there were two dressing stalls. A single, large oval shaped mirror was on the wall beside them with a round raised platform in front of the mirror.

Lily walked over to a bench sitting across from the stalls and indicated for the both of them to have a seat.

"Please, girls, have a seat and I will be right back with the most exquisite dress you've been looking for!" Lily said cheerfully and walked away.

"Exquisite..." Alexia repeated as she looked around. "This place is pretty snazzy, isn't it? She's really nice too. I can't wait to see the dress she's going to bring back!" Alexia said as she rested her gigantic dress bag on one side of the bench and sat down next to Amanda.

After a few minutes, Lily showed up with a color that Amanda didn't even consider trying on.

Black. Solid Black.

"I don't know about you, but black is always very classy and not to mention, sexy! I think you should give this a try and see what you think." Lily explained as she slid the dress off the hanger.

"I'm not sure…" Amanda went to talk when Alexia cut her off.

"Oh, come on, trying on anything at this point might help. Don't be picky and just try it on. I have to admit that black is a little heavy for prom, but why not?"

Amanda looked at the dress as Lily held it up for all of them to see.

"Fine." Amanda said and took the dress from Lily's hands.

"That a girl!" Alexia said and smiled as she looked up at Lily. "Sorry about that, sometimes she's just so stubborn and difficult!"

"It's no problem at all. There's been worse that I've dealt with. This is nothing." Lily said and winked at Alexia.

"So, how long has this store been here? I don't think I've seen it here before, but then again I haven't been to this mall in a while." Alexia asked.

"Oh, yes, we just opened last month. We figured what the hell? Being that it's prom season, we figured it'd be the most suitable time to open our shop."

Amanda unlocked the stall door and stepped out in the black dress.

The dress had thin straps that wrapped around her neck like a halter and crossed down her back. The dress was form fitting and outlined the curves of Amanda's middle before it flared down past her bottom and touched the floor.

"You look... awesome!" Alexia said. "It's really nice!"

Lily walked closer to Amanda as she stepped up onto the platform and glanced into the mirror.

"If you chose this one, you'd be the *envy* of the prom!" Lily said encouragingly with a big smile.

"I guess, but I think black makes me look too... pale. Don't I look pale?" Amanda asked Alexia.

"Turn around and face me so I can get a better look." Alexia said.

As Amanda turned around, she noticed the bald man had been standing behind Alexia, observing the three of them. She wasn't sure how long he'd been standing there.

"No, no. Lily, this dress is too dark for such an... ivory beauty."

His voice caught Alexia by surprise and she jumped to her feet.

"Oh! I didn't know you were behind me! You came out of nowhere." Alexia said.

The bald man appeared to be in his thirties and had to have stood just over six feet tall. He was dressed in a light gray suit and a white tie, giving him an appearance of an ideal upstanding gentleman who might be ready to attend a wedding or formal cocktail party. His piercing ice blue eyes watched and his brilliant white teeth appeared when he smiled. He was extremely attractive and very polite, making him all the more appealing.

The man seemed to be carefully observing Amanda while stroking his chin, as if he were contemplating something.

"Lily, I think I have just the thing for this beautiful..." the man paused and narrowed his gaze at Amanda, then turned to Lily. "... girl. I think the black may take away the glow about her. It's a little too overwhelming, don't you agree?"

The man's gaze shifted from Lily to Amanda and it could have taken her breath away. She could already see that it had taken away Alexia's. Alexia just stood there and hadn't said a single word.

"Yes. I think it's a little much." Amanda managed to squeeze out without sounding too caught up in the moment.

Lily looked at the salesman and Amanda could have sworn she saw her roll her eyes at him. She didn't mean to offend Lily but Amanda just wasn't fond of the dress enough to buy it for prom.

It was too... black.

"Okay, then. Take it off." Lily demanded and gestured impatiently for Amanda to go back into the dressing stall.

In that one moment, Lily's attitude had altered drastically and Amanda could only assume that maybe the man was her boss.

Maybe she had failed to pick the right dress? Maybe she didn't like the man's criticism?

Amanda wasn't sure.

As Amanda changed out of the dress, she could hear Alexia anxiously rummaging through her small purse, probably in search of a lip gloss while the man had gone to get the dress.

Amanda laughed to herself and whispered through the dressing room door.

"You know, Gregg wouldn't like you getting all pretty for another guy. Especially some salesman!"

"Shut up! There's no harm in putting on some lip gloss… just because my lips are dry." Alexia replied quickly.

"Oh, please." Amanda laughed.

"He's coming back…" Alexia said and shoved her lip gloss back into her bag.

Amanda listened as she hung the black dress over the door, ready for the next gown.

"Oh, wow. Amanda, wait till you see this one!"

The salesman slid the black dress off the door and replaced it with a ruby red colored gown.

—◦◦◦—

Ruby Red.

Amanda stood on the platform and observed herself in the mirror. She could see the salesman and Alexia looking on in the reflection, both with an approving expression on their faces.

Amanda had never seen a dress quite like it and clung to her body as if it had been made just for her.

It was truly a rich, ruby red color and it complimented her complexion beautifully. It was almost velvety looking with the way it moved in the light.

"What's it made of?" Alexia asked, dumbfounded by its elegance.

"Silk. The finest of any kind." The salesman said and Amanda felt herself blush as he admired her in the mirror.

Amanda turned and examined the backside of the dress to find it open and the fabric dropping down to reveal the small of her back. The dress flowed down to the floor like a cascading river of rubies.

Wait until Mitch sees…

"Timeless and special. It leaves you glowing. You and that dress are one of a kind." The salesman said and headed over to the register.

His choice of words made Amanda turn around with curiosity.

It was coincidence, right?

"What?" Amanda asked softly watching him walk away.

"What a compliment!" Alexia said, pretending to fan herself down. "I wish Gregg would talk to me like that!"

Amanda brushed off the salesman's interesting choice of words and looked back at herself in the mirror. She couldn't help but come to terms with the fact that she loved the gown.

"Well, this is it!" Amanda smiled and glanced at Alexia in the reflection.

"Yes! I couldn't agree more but I have to admit, I thought we'd never find it!" Alexia said and dramatically sighed with relief.

Amanda went back into the stall and changed back into her top and jean shorts. She neatly placed the gown onto its proper hanger as she took a moment to admire the silky gown.

Amanda opened the stall door to find Lily waiting a few feet away from her while Alexia was up at the register babbling on to the salesman.

Such a flirt… so typical…

"I'll ring you up at the register. Are you satisfied with the dress *he* picked out for you?"

She no longer seemed irritated and was more than willing to assist Amanda with anything else she needed.

"I love it, actually. Thank you for your help though, the black one was nice." Amanda said, trying to be polite.

Lily took the dress from Amanda's hands and turned around quickly as she headed toward the register with Amanda following behind her. It was hard to get a good read on the saleswoman and at times it seemed like her mood kept switching on and off at random.

"Oh, please, no need to say anything of the sort. I prefer black, but that's just me. Red is still a great color and it seems to suit you." Lily said as she rounded the corner of the counter.

The salesman was busy counting receipts as Alexia continued to try and flirt with him. It was clear that he was not interested but Alexia never knew when to quit at times.

"You know, gray suits are my favorite, I think they always look good on…"

Amanda nudged Alexia, forcing Alexia to quit talking. Alexia tossed Amanda a disappointed expression for disrupting her opportunity.

"Are you interested in shoes as well?" Lily asked after ringing up the dress and covering it up in a sheer gown bag.

"Oh! You need shoes, Amanda!" Alexia said.

"I have just the thing for you."

The salesman placed the receipts on the counter and walked over to the shoe display on the other side of the small store. He snagged the shoes and walked back over to the counter, putting down the shoes before them.

The heels were the same shade of red with a small gold chain lining the tips.

"Well, what do you think?" Lily asked impatiently.

"These are so hot!" Alexia answered for Amanda.

"They're not only hot, they're the latest trend. Better snag them up because they're our last pair." Lily said, insisting that they take the heels as quickly as possible.

"We'll take them!" Alexia said.

The salesman smiled and they couldn't help but find it irresistibly infectious and smiled back, blushing wildly.

Once the dress and shoes were paid for, Amanda and Alexia headed for the exit of the store when the salesman called out to them.

"Have a wonderful time at prom!"

Alexia giggled as she waved and they walked back into the mall and headed for the exit toward the car.

"He was so hot! I mean I've never really been into bald guys, but he was definitely an exception to the rule! You know what? We didn't even get his name." Alexia said, frowning and disappointed.

"You're *lucky* we didn't get his name, because the next thing you would've been begging for was his number!" Amanda said and laughed as Alexia bumped into her on purpose.

"Oh, come on, I wouldn't have gone *that* far, besides Gregg is still my man. Watcher or no watcher." Alexia winked as she hauled her dress and bags over her shoulder.

"Shh!"

"Oh, come on! It's not like anyone will know what it means anyway." Alexia said. "Oh! Just so you know, I made our hair and makeup appointments at Sheri's at Sea Grove on Saturday. Since money's not a problem this time, I will not have you do your own hair like you did last year for junior prom."

"But..."

"Nope, it's senior prom and we're going all out! Sheri's always does such an amazing job so I thought it'd be the place to go! You're coming whether you like it or not."

Alexia wouldn't let Amanda get away without getting her hair done professionally this time. Amanda didn't think she did such a bad job by herself for junior prom but Alexia complained that it was too plain and boring. Admittedly, Amanda had only added a hairclip and figured it shouldn't have been a huge deal given that she was going without a date but Alexia wasn't convinced. Now that Mitch was in her life, Alexia would make sure Amanda was looking good at all times and especially the senior prom with her first date, ever.

"Okay, fine." Amanda agreed and smiled.

"Anyway, I don't know what was going on with that Lily girl and her mood swings but *he* was definitely something else, wasn't he?" Alexia said dreamily.

"Yeah, he was something else." Amanda said thoughtfully as they walked side by side out the mall exit.

Chapter 11

HAUNTED

$\mathcal{T}$he few nights leading up to prom had been nothing but torture.

No word from Mitch and the dreams had been reborn.

The nightmares had started again and she couldn't understand why. She could only assume that it could be herself consciousness, punishing herself for forcing Mitch out again and not having any communication with him.

God, she missed him. Her heart yearned everlastingly for him.

But she kept reminding herself that balance was more important. She was confident that it would eventually bring them together again.

Each morning she would wake up, damp with sweat and a sense of fear in the back of her mind. She'd wake up, distraught and disappointed with only a vague memory of what she had experienced.

Darkness, fire, heat, and that frightening river of blood.

Amanda remembered back to the first time the river had swept her away in her dream. She couldn't fight the continuous flow, let alone catch a single breath until that one moment.

Someone had reached in and grabbed her, saving her from drowning.

She still didn't know who it could have been. The only thing she knew was that it wasn't Mitch. It couldn't have been. Mitch had even admitted that the figure in the dream wasn't him which left them both questioning who would have saved her.

Amanda sat up in her bed to find the sun coming in through her window and Oreo lying by her feet, eyes wide with curiosity.

The blankets had been down past her waist, indicating that she had to have been squirming about in her bed that night.

She assumed that he must have scooted down to the end of the bed away from her, afraid of being forced off and onto the floor.

Amanda closed her eyes and tried to focus on the vague memory of her dream that night. There had been one significant difference. She remembered kicking and screaming, relentlessly fighting the river's rapids and when she'd manage to peek up above the flow, she recalled having seen strange dark figures along the river's edges.

They simply stood there, motionless as they watched her struggle and suffer. They were like a blur in her mind.

Blur...

Amanda opened her eyes and glanced over to the mirror on her dresser.

She recalled seeing something dark in the dressing room mirror while prom dress shopping with Alexia. It only appeared to be some sort of dark blur or shadow but before she had managed to get a good look, it had vanished.

Amanda wondered if it really was her imagination playing games with her. She knew that she hadn't been feeling too confident with her decision to let go of Mitch for the time being and she thought that maybe it was just taking a toll on her. It was impossible to be able to tell, given the supernatural things she had become aware of.

Mitch had also explained that Demons could create nightmares and communicate through them.

Was someone trying to communicate with her?

Amanda huffed with frustration because she knew that there was still much for her to learn but the figures seemed to haunt her memory once she remembered them.

It was more than frightening and she frowned as she tried to dismiss the images in her head.

Amanda leaned forward and grabbed Oreo, cradling him in her arms as she snuggled up close to his face. Just having him there made her feel more at peace after having another horrible dream.

He licked her face and she giggled quietly.

"You always know how to make me smile." Amanda said and kissed the little dog on his forehead before placing him back on her blanket.

Amanda leaned over to her nightstand and picked up her phone. It was Saturday, ten o'clock in the morning and she had two missed calls.

Her stomach dropped at the hope of seeing Mitch's name on her phone.

She could only hope...

But she scrolled through her phone to find that both were from Alexia.

Amanda sighed as she placed her phone back onto the nightstand and plopped back down onto her bed, pulling the covers over her head.

It was the day of prom.

Chapter 12

PLAIN AND SIMPLE

*A*fter forcing herself to get out of bed, Amanda tossed her hair into a pony tail and wandered downstairs to find the front door open and Nan sitting out on the porch.

She opened the screen door and walked outside, yawning and stretching from side to side.

"Good morning, Angel." Nan said as she calmly swayed back and forth in her rocking chair with a book in her lap. Oreo was lying at her feet as he always did.

"Morning, Nan."

"Beautiful day, today. I'd say it's just right for prom, wouldn't you say?"

Amanda sighed and looked blankly at her grandmother.

"Oh, Amanda, I don't understand why you won't just have an open mind and open your heart to a fun opportunity. I understand you think it's all pointless now, but you should go ahead and enjoy yourself."

"Prom and Alexia aren't the things that are bothering me, it's…" Amanda hesitated before continuing as her grandmother waited for her to finish her thought. "It's Mitch."

Her grandmother simply shook her head.

"Amanda, you already know my opinion about him, but what happened this time? Are you alright?"

"We had an argument and he just doesn't get it sometimes. I pretty much told him I wanted some time for myself to work with my Light. He didn't understand because he's so stubborn." Amanda said as she crossed her arms with frustration.

"Maybe he didn't *want* to understand. Selfishness is in his nature and you, more than anyone should have realized that by now. Besides, you know, stubbornness is a natural quality that you both share."

"Thanks, Nan but seriously, I don't know what to do. I know you don't like to hear it but I care about him a lot. It's just so hard to make things work when there's a part of me that is so different from him."

"I see. What made you consider spending time apart from him to begin with?"

"Alexia and Gregg introduced me to a new Watcher, Luca. He seemed to understand what I've been going through and recommended that I should try to balance things out." Amanda said, looking back up at her grandmother.

"He told you to try to maintain a balance?"

"Yes, but it's so hard to do when..." Amanda tried to explain just as Nan finished her thought.

"...when you're with him all the time?" Nan said with a warm grin.

"Yes. I mean we went through this before and bad things happened when we were apart. But I just feel like I had to take time for myself. I know that you, Gregg and Alexia have been trying to tell me that I've been spending too much time with him but maybe I just needed someone from the outside to tell me. It got me thinking and it just felt good to hear it from someone I didn't already know."

"I think you are absolutely right. I understand when you have family or friends who are biased trying to tell you what to do and how to do it can be irritating. And I know you so well Amanda, being stubborn has been a quality within you, even before any of this happened. But being stubborn isn't always a bad thing, standing your ground is part of a strength you have. Not everyone has the ability to voice how they feel. You speak your mind and that's very important. You don't give up and that's a very good thing. But sometimes it's also a good thing to have an open mind."

"I guess you're right." Amanda said as she picked up Oreo into her arms for some comfort. She snuggled her face into his smooth coat and closed her eyes.

"So, my dear, are you worried that Mitch might not show up to go with you to the prom?" Nan asked.

Amanda opened her eyes and pulled the dog away from her face, cradling the dog in her arms.

"I guess. I just haven't heard from him and we're all supposed to go tonight." Amanda said as she tried not to let the lump in her throat get any bigger than it already was. Just the thought of him not showing up made her stomach queasy.

"Listen, I'm sure he'll show up. I think that if he truly cares, he will be here for you. Just remember sweetheart, he's a demon. I know that you know all of this already but I also know that you see him as something more. The heart is a fragile thing and sometimes it can deceive you. That is why it's very important to have an open mind while following your heart. It's kind of like the balance you're trying to create between darkness and light. You should follow and listen to your heart but remember to also think logically. Love is a beautiful blessing in life but it can also be complicated. The Lord gives us challenges to learn from and love can certainly be one of those challenges."

Amanda took a deep breath as she took in all of her grandmother's advice. She gently placed the dog down by her feet and stood back up to look at her grandmother.

"Thanks, Nan. I don't know what I'd do without you."

"It's what I am here for, darling. Now, go out with Alexia and get ready for your prom," The elderly woman said and smiled at Amanda as she opened the book in her lap.

Amanda smiled and ran back inside to call Alexia. The advice from her grandmother seemed to have lifted her spirits and her grandmother's wisdom always seemed to brighten her day.

Have an open mind but follow your heart.

Could it really be that simple?

Amanda smiled and she noted the thought in her mind, making sure never to let it go.

Mitch would show up because he loved her. It was as plain and simple as that. She always had the tendency to make things bigger than they really were.

She just hoped her grandmother was right once again. Nan's wisdom never seemed to fail her and she just had to loosen up a bit.

Amanda could only hope that he wouldn't let something as simple as an argument stand between what they had.

She had to stop *feeling* like every moment that they spent apart was the end of the world.

Chapter 13

BURN

𝒯he snagging and pulling was starting to annoy Amanda as she watched the hairstylist in the mirror.

Later that afternoon, Amanda met up with Alexia and they drove over to Sheri's at Sea Grove. There were only a few hours remaining before the limo would pick them up to take them to prom. Amanda thought that a limo was a bit much but Alexia had insisted and her parents willingly paid to make sure their daughter got what she wanted.

The sun shone through the salon's large windows, spanning from the ceiling to the floor. Customers entering the salon were greeted by Sheri, herself at the wooden podium in the front where the register and a few seats were located along the windows.

One side of the salon had multiple silver shelving units containing only the best hair products and hair supplies while the other side was lined up with all of the stylists individual stations.

The salon was decorated beautifully with dark cherry wood flooring and matching cabinets along the almond colored walls. The salon was upscale but still maintained a cozy and rich, rustic ambiance.

The stylist continued to brush out and pull down her hair with a hot curling iron as the faded memory of Ravish dragging her along the boardwalk by her hair surfaced in her mind. Amanda recalled coming in and out of consciousness and the throbbing of her head from the impact. The more the brush pulled and the curling iron clamped down, the more bothersome Amanda started to feel.

Despite visiting Sea Grove throughout her childhood, the oceanic town didn't quite feel the same since that night. It had changed everything and to simply shake off the horrible memories of Ravish, the rollercoaster and the life threatening situation, it wasn't that easy.

Amanda closed her eyes for a moment and tried to force out the memory before it got the best of her, but the brink had been reached.

"I'm sorry," Amanda blurted out, "but can you just be a little gentler? I... um, I have a sensitive scalp." Amanda asked as politely as she could. She had to make it known or else she would've been uncomfortable the entire time.

"Oh! I'm so sorry, I didn't mean to hurt you. I'll take it easy."

The petite young hairstylist apologized and smiled before starting to brush once again. The girl was obviously new but only the best stylists in the area were hired at Sheri's.

Amanda smiled as she glanced over to see Alexia flipping through a magazine containing all sorts of hairstyles.

"I think this one would be perfect." Alexia said and pointed to a model in the book and showed it to the male stylist.

"Whatever you want, sweetie. Look at this gorgeous hair! You can do anything with this!"

The stylist bragged about Alexia's beautiful red hair and she beamed with a big smile and thanked the young man.

Amanda looked back into the mirror at her reflection and jumped in her chair at the sight that she saw. It caught her so off guard, she could have screamed.

Or thought she saw, again.

The hairstylist jumped backwards, startled by Amanda's sudden movement. She clumsily tripped over her own feet as her brush dropped to the floor.

A black blur...

Amanda had seen the same dark figure that she'd seen when they had gone prom dress shopping at Phillip's.

But just as she'd seen it, it disappeared once again.

The large, dark figure had been standing directly behind her and next to the stylist.

After a moment, Amanda exhaled after she realized it had scared her so much that she had been holding her breath.

"Are you okay, sweetie?" The stylist asked cautiously as she picked her brush up off the floor.

"Didn't you see that?" Amanda asked, turning around and looking directly where it had been standing.

"See what?" The girl looked around, confused. "Are you okay?"

"What's wrong, Amanda?" Alexia asked, turning to her friend but Amanda couldn't answer.

She had no idea what she was seeing. This time it had been incredibly close and it made it easier for her to see some sort of detail. The only thing she noticed this time was the figure was dark because it had been some sort of covering, similar to that of a heavy cloak. But that was all she could make out, given how fast the image came and went.

Amanda found herself just as confused as the stylist and turned back to face her reflection.

No dark figure, but the fear refused to leave her gut.

Something wasn't quite right but she couldn't quite pin it down.

Amanda sighed and glanced over at Alexia.

"I'm fine, I just thought I saw something. Maybe I'm just tired." Amanda said, making up anything she could to make up for her outburst.

"Well, you better wake up soon because prom is only in a few more hours!" Alexia said and turned her focus back into the magazine in her lap.

"I'm sorry." Amanda said to the stylist through the mirror.

"It's alright, you're just lucky I didn't have the curling iron in my hand. Someone could've gotten burned real bad."

Ironically enough, the dark figure burned an image into her mind and she had tried to focus. The figure was unusually familiar but she couldn't understand why. She knew for sure that it wasn't her imagination this time.

This was real.

It was time to talk to him without fail.

Mitch.

Chapter 14

F⊕RSAKEN

*L*ater that evening, Amanda was in her room getting ready and prom was only an hour away.

After getting their hair done at Sheri's, Amanda had gone back home to change and wait for Alexia to come with the limo that would bring them to the prom.

Mitch was bound to show up at any moment and she was incredibly anxious to speak with him about what happened only hours before. She needed to tell him about the dark figures that were haunting her and ask him if he knew anything about them.

Amanda slid her feet into the crimson heels laced with the small gold chains along the toe. They definitely added a nice touch to the shoes and they glimmered each time the light hit them.

She let the dress fall to the floor, covering them as she walked over to the elongated mirror in the corner of her bedroom.

Amanda hesitated and closed her eyes before stepping into the view of her reflection.

Mirrors were going to become a phobia if those figures were going to keep showing up without notice.

Please don't be there...

When she stepped forward and opened her eyes, she was relieved to see only herself looking in the reflection. Amanda couldn't believe how different but surprisingly beautiful she looked.

Her hair was parted further to the side as it swooped down just past her eye. The rest of her hair was loosely curled and pinned up in the back with a few strands falling down on the sides.

A hint of smoky eye shadow, dusted with gold shimmer made her green eyes stand out nicely. Black eye liner and mascara added a final touch while a hint of pink blush gave her a rose kissed glow.

Wait until he sees...

The thought of Mitch seeing the way she looked made her smile and she spun around playfully, twirling the silky red dress all around her. She was surprised to find herself so enthralled in being dressed up and she couldn't help but enjoy the fact that she truly felt beautiful and it was all for Mitch.

He'll forget about everything that happened once he sees...

A faint knock came from her bedroom door as Nan peeked into the room. Amanda stopped spinning and when she saw her grandmother, she smiled shyly.

"Well?" Amanda asked.

Nan walked over to her granddaughter as they both turned to face the mirror and admired Amanda's appearance. The elderly woman placed her hands gently on Amanda's shoulders.

"There are no words. You're a dream. An Angel." Nan said as Amanda felt herself blush at the compliment.

"Thanks, Nan. It's strange getting all dressed up like this but I think I actually kind of like it." Amanda said beaming with excitement. "They should be here any minute."

Before Nan could say another word, a knock was heard on the front door downstairs.

"Well, that's probably your date." Nan said as Amanda took a deep breath before turning and heading toward her bedroom door.

"Amanda..." Nan stopped Amanda before she could leave. "I love you. Have a good time tonight."

"I love you too, Nan." Amanda said, taking in the moment before rushing out into the hall. She rushed down the stairs almost tripping on her heels before reaching the front door.

The thought of seeing Mitch again made her heart pound faster in her chest as she grabbed the door and swung it open.

Her smiled disappeared when she realized who had been knocking on the door.

"Hey! Oh my God, you look amazing!" Alexia said.

It wasn't Mitch...

Alexia admired Amanda from head to toe as Amanda stood, frozen in the door way, speechless and confused.

He should've been here by now...

Amanda looked beyond Alexia in search of him to find only the white limo sitting in the street. Mitch was nowhere to be found.

Where was he?

Alexia noticed Amanda's expression and looked around, following her gaze to see what Amanda was searching for.

"What's wrong? What is it?"

"Is he in the limo?" Amanda asked, hoping her friend would say yes.

"Who? Wait, where's Mitch?" Alexia asked with a concerned look on her face. "He's not here?"

"No, he's... he's not."

Amanda could feel her stomach drop to the floor and the overwhelming sensation of tears started to form behind her eyes.

"He's not here." Amanda said breathlessly over and over again as she felt anxiety take hold of her. "He's not here."

Her breath started to quicken and her legs weakened significantly, causing her to clumsily fall to her knees. She could feel her wings droop lifelessly onto the floor behind her and her heart felt as if it had been crushed.

"Whoa, Amanda, calm down. Maybe he's just a little late. We'll wait a little longer for him. It's okay." Alexia said as she knelt down beside Amanda, trying her best to comfort her.

"What happened? Is Amanda alright?"

Nan hurried down the stairs as she descended upon the scene to find her granddaughter distraught.

"Mitch isn't here, he didn't come." Alexia said. "She's really upset. I think she's having an anxiety attack."

"Oh, Amanda…"

Nan came around and helped her granddaughter to her feet as she helped Amanda over to the couch.

Alexia and Nan sat on either side of her as Amanda continued to sob uncontrollably and tears rolled endlessly down her cheeks.

"Sweetheart, he might still need some time to get over your argument. Don't give up hope." Nan said and lifted Amanda's chin to face her.

"But, it's prom. I did all of this for him."

"I know it meant a lot to you, but you should also do all of this for yourself, not just for someone else. Don't let this discourage you."

Her grandmother's energy usually had a tendency to help calm her and put her at ease but the situation was too overwhelming for Amanda to feel anything else but grief.

She loved him.

Amanda not only wanted him there, but she needed him.

How could he do this to her?

"Nan's right, Amanda. I know he means a lot to you and I mean, I think he cares about you a lot but who knows what he's thinking right now. You shouldn't let this bring you down so hard. I know he's your first boyfriend but hopefully this is just a bump in the road right now." Alexia said and squeezed Amanda's hand as she wrapped her other arm around her shoulders. "Just take a moment to calm down. Just breathe."

"Is it over? Did he really just do this to me?" Amanda asked as she wiped her tears to find some makeup smudged on her palms.

Amanda couldn't comprehend the reality of the situation. It felt as if she were having yet another nightmare.

The worst nightmare.

She could only think of what her grandmother had told her.

What could she really expect when she was dating a Demon?

He was a creature with an unexpected temper and unbelievable stubbornness.

She was right.

"How could I be so stupid?" Amanda asked herself out loud.

"Are you kidding me?" Alexia asked as she pulled back and looked Amanda directly in the face. "You are not stupid! If anything, he's stupid because he obviously has no idea how amazing you are. He just completely burned his own ass with Hellfire for what he did."

Nan tossed Alexia a disappointing glance.

"Okay, I'm sorry for my choice of words, Nan, but I'm just venting right now. Listen, Amanda I know you're hurt but it's not your fault. You were only trying to do the right thing and he walked out on you. I just think you should give it time and he'll see exactly what he did. Then he'll come back on his hands and knees, apologizing and begging to get you back. You pretty much told me yourself that it was a misunderstanding."

Amanda nodded her head and took a deep breath, attempting to calm down. After a few moments, Amanda wiped her face and managed to steady her breathing.

"Now what do I do?" Amanda asked, feeling hopeless.

"Well, you already know what I think. I think we should clean up your makeup, hop in the limo and go have a great night at prom. Forget about Mitch and let's just go have a good time." Alexia said encouragingly.

"I guess." Amanda said, knowing that despite what happened, she couldn't break her promise to Alexia.

"Besides, I have a back up date for you. I mean he's kind of going by himself too, so it could work out, right?" Alexia winked.

"Who?" Amanda asked cautiously.

Just then, a knock came from the living room door way and the three looked up to find Gregg neatly dressed in his tuxedo. Amanda saw that his vest and tie matched the blue color of Alexia's ball gown. She then noticed someone else standing in the foyer behind him but her smudged makeup, she couldn't make out who it was.

Her heart jumped at the hope that it was Mitch.

"Is everything okay?" Gregg asked before entering the room.

Amanda started to wipe her eyes so she could get a good look at who was behind Gregg.

"We're fine, babe." Alexia said. "Unfortunately, Mitch won't be joining us."

It wasn't Mitch...

Once Gregg saw the situation and how upset Amanda appeared to be, he hesitated, unsure of how to respond to Alexia's comment.

"Okay, well, we'll be waiting outside whenever you're ready. Come on, Luca."

The two Watchers walked swiftly out of the foyer and onto the front porch toward the limo.

"What's Luca doing here?" Amanda asked.

"Well, we invited him to tag along because he's part of the group now. Maybe... you could be his date?" Alexia said nudging Amanda playfully trying to lighten the mood.

"I think date is a strong word." Amanda said frowning.

"Ok, well maybe not a date but a friend who is also without a date who needs a friend to hang out with?" Alexia said, knowing she sounded silly. "Does that sound better?"

Amanda wasn't in any mood to argue or reject the offer. She was open to any idea, whatever it would take to possibly make herself feel better if her friends thought it would.

Just go with it. What other choice was there anyway?

"Fine." Amanda said as Alexia pulled her back up onto her feet.

Amanda could feel her eyes had puffed up and they were slightly stinging from the abundance of tears.

"Amanda dear, don't go out if you don't want to. If you want to stay home, it's okay." Nan said before Amanda could walk out of the room.

Amanda appreciated her grandmother's concern but she couldn't let her best friend down. Sometimes if you made promises, you had to keep them, regardless of the circumstances.

She wouldn't let Alexia down.

"Thanks, Nan. But I think I'll be okay. Don't worry, I just have to keep my head up and follow my heart like someone once told me. And my heart's telling me that I need to spend time with my friends."

The elderly woman smiled and appreciated hearing that her granddaughter understood the advice she had given.

"Okay, then. Go have fun."

Chapter 15

DRAGGED

The sun was setting as he watched the wind blow across the grass.

Mitch sat in the field, with his arms wrapped around his knees as he watched the sun spread its light across the sky just before succumbing to the embrace of the horizon.

He slid his cell phone from the pocket of his black jeans and noticed the time. There were minutes left before he'd have to leave to go meet with Amanda before the prom.

Mitch never met up with Gregg to get a tuxedo for what he thought was the most ridiculous event, but all he knew was that he wouldn't let her go with the new Watcher she had told him about.

Luca.

The Watcher had some nerve…

Mitch already despised the Watcher for trying to lead Amanda astray from him. The Demon couldn't even fathom what were to happen if they ever came face to face.

Did she really want to be away from him? Why couldn't she understand that bad things happened when they were apart?

The memory of their argument almost left a bitter taste in his mouth but he wasn't going to let it come between he and Amanda. She still needed to be protected and there was no way in hell that he would let anything happen to her. Even though he had left furious and insanely frustrated with the choice she'd made, he wouldn't let Amanda slip away from him that easily. Not by an idea that some Watcher tossed into her head.

Space...

Mitch grimaced at the concept of being away from her and it made him sick to his human stomach. In his mind, space was the last thing they needed.

But despite the fact that he was insanely angry with her, the truth of the matter was that he loved her.

Period.

Mitch knew he was lucky enough to even grasp the notion of what love meant and how it felt. That never happened with Demons and it never would but by some miracle, it had happened and it happened it him.

He simply couldn't let that go. It made him feel so different, so extraordinary, so... blessed.

Mitch closed his eyes and he could almost feel the soft touch of her lips kissing his. Those moments were what he loved most and the memory of it always warmed him to the very core of his demonic soul.

For days, he'd been longing to touch her, hold her, kiss her. Aside from being consumed in anger, he tried so very hard to respect her. He didn't have to stay out of her life when she commanded it, but he did it anyway.

For her.

He was hers and she was his. There was nothing more essential than that.

Suddenly, he heard a faint sound interrupt his reverie.

He wasn't alone.

His eyes burst wide open and realized the sound was coming from behind him and it sounded as if someone was clearing their throat.

He stood up quickly to face whoever was behind him and froze in place when he noticed he was in fact surrounded.

Mitch looked around cautiously to find tall cloaked figures standing motionless in a large circle, preventing him from escaping.

And he knew exactly who they were.

The Seven Deadly Sins.

He saw a Demon walk out from behind one the Sins.

Ravish.

Only this time, the wicked Demon's appearance was different. Her ensemble was dark and wild, her hair frazzled and disheveled.

"Well, you're looking good, Ravish. Have a melt down or something?" Mitch asked boldly as he stood his ground and prepared himself for a fight.

"Wrong. Guess again." Ravish said, not amused.

"Wait, let's see. You stuck those little black nails into an electrical socket?" Mitch asked.

He chuckled at the joke but stopped when he noticed one very different article of jewelry she was wearing. He knew it very well and it didn't belong to her.

His ring.

"Very funny, Malicious. You always had such a sense of humor." Ravish said as she crept in closer to him. "No, actually I was thrown away and banished by an Angel, remember?"

"Oh, yes! How could I forget." Mitch said sarcastically. "So, what is this? You brought a whole party with you this time?"

"I wouldn't call it a party, Malicious." Ravish said, stopping only a few feet away from him. "You see, a certain someone kept a secret that shouldn't have been kept, especially from *him*. I'd rather call it your funeral."

"I don't think so." Mitch said through his teeth as he clenched his fists tightly.

"Oh, I think so." Ravish hissed in his face. "Light 'em up!"

Before a single word could be spoken, the Sins let out a bone shattering screech as Hellfire burst outward from under the hoods of their cloaks, engulfing Mitch in a fury of Hellfire.

Within seconds, they were all gone, only to have left behind a charred, smoldering crater.

Chapter 16

THE PR⊕Ⅲ

The hour drive to prom felt as though it took forever. The music was blasting and the neon lights lining the mini bar of the limo shimmered as they blended into a rainbow of colors.

Once Alexia had cleaned up Amanda's make up smudges, they all climbed into the stretch limo and left for the prom. Amanda tried as hard as she could to brush off how low her spirit was but it was difficult to ignore. Alexia kept snapping pictures the entire way there with her phone but Amanda couldn't muster any energy to smile in any single one of them.

"Hey." Luca said and nudged her gently. The Watcher had been sitting beside her the entire time and he couldn't help but notice that their every attempt to make her smile didn't seem to do much of anything. "Everything will be okay."

Amanda let out a deep breath, trying to shake off her sense of depression but she felt like she couldn't look him in the face just yet.

"Thanks." Amanda said and started twiddling her thumbs in her lap.

Amanda could feel the limo coming to a slow crawl as she looked up through the tinted window to see an abundance of lights appearing through the trees.

The Villa de Escaparse.

The limo had begun to line up with all the other cars outside the venue.

"We're here!" Alexia squealed as she scooted over to the car door excitedly.

As they exited the limo one by one, Luca outstretched his open palm, kindly offering to help her out of the limo. Amanda hesitated before deciding it was harmless as she slipped her hand into his and he gently pulled her up and out with ease.

Amanda landed carefully on her heels, as she made sure to maintain her balance without clumsily falling over. She glanced up at the extravagant setting before following her friends inside.

The senior prom was being held at Villa de Escaparse, one the most popular places for any kind of event from weddings to proms. A higher end villa with raving reviews about the location, service and the food.

The massive Tuscan adobe styled mansion sat on the end of a cul-de-sac as the drive way wrapped around a considerably large fountain lit up with a cerulean glow. Small white decorative lights twinkled and illuminated the high rounded archways at the front entrance as students made their way inside.

The entire structure looked as though it were right out of a vacation magazine and there weren't many places such as the Villa de Escaparse in New Jersey.

"Shall we?"

Amanda looked beside her to find Luca standing upright and extending his elbow, in an attempt to take Amanda's arm in his. She realized that she had been so distracted and down that his appearance didn't seem to faze her until that moment. Amanda took notice of his debonair demeanor and with his black tuxedo and pearl colored vest and tie. His blonde hair was slick back and his dazzling blue eyes looked down, directly at her as he patiently waited for her response.

Amanda admired his uniquely colored eyes but her heart was wishing that she was looking into the black ones with which she loved so much.

Don't think about him…

She tossed the thought away from her mind as she looked back at Luca, deciding to try and enjoy herself for the night.

Amanda appreciated the kind gesture and figured what harm could it do?

She slid her arm through his as they followed Gregg and Alexia through the archway and inside.

As they walked through the expansive foyer, students filled the room as they signed in at the table to get their tickets and cast their votes for prom court, queen and king.

The foyer had beautifully tiled flooring and a large staircase that led up the doors that would grant then entry into the main room.

A massive vintage clock with roman numerals hung above the main doors to where the prom would take place up on the balcony. Intricately detailed columns held up the beautifully painted ceilings as the students wondered around admiring every inch of the main lobby.

As they among the many students, Amanda looked up and noticed the mural painted on the ceiling high above them.

The sun and its rays penetrated the wispy painted clouds and blue birds swooped through the air. The uplifting painting made her smile as she admired it from below when she caught Luca looking at her from the corner of her eye.

"What?" Amanda asked caught off guard.

"I didn't say anything." Luca said casually.

"But you were looking at me…" Amanda said as she crossed her arms, suddenly feeling slightly insecure.

"What? I can't look at you?" Luca asked and smiled at her. "You look amazing."

Amanda didn't expect the overwhelming compliment. She hadn't heard anyone compliment her like that other than Mitch or her grandmother. She hadn't known Luca for long and the compliment surprised her.

But before Amanda could respond, it was their turn to sign in and cast their votes.

Amanda could care less about prom court but she knew it meant the world to Alexia.

Amanda read down the brief list of competitors and found Alexia's name toward the bottom. Amanda checked off her best friend and then checked off people at random for the remaining nominations.

Once they were finished, the four of them were handed their tickets and headed up the grand staircase.

Alexia and Amanda walked side by side, climbing the stairs as the Watchers followed behind them.

"Oh my God, I hope I make prom court! I mean queen would be even more amazing!" Alexia said, beaming with excitement.

"It would definitely be cool if that happened. I hope so!" Amanda said, hoping for the best for Alexia.

They came to a halt midway up the stairs among many other students waiting to enter into the main room. The anxious students were chattering up a storm with excitement as they waited in the massive line.

The clock struck the top of the hour and the large wooden doors slowly opened, allowing the students to enter.

Once they were through the doorway, the massive room left everyone in awe.

The floor was a beautiful tan and white marble and a magnificent crystal chandelier hung at the center of the room, above the dance floor. Thick ribbons swooped throughout the room in the school's colors of black and orange.

It was truly a sight to behold.

If only Mitch was here...

A DJ was set up in the corner with music already playing loudly as the bass bounced around the room.

Large round tables were set up surrounding the dance floor and a raised platform was at the head of the room with a microphone stand.

"Wow!" Alexia said, practically speechless.

Amanda looked at her ticket that displayed a number three, assigning them to the proper table.

"We're at table three." Amanda said as she looked around the room and found their table located right along the side of the dance floor. "Over there."

The four of them made their way over to the table and took a seat. Amanda sat down beside Alexia and watched as her friend whipped out her phone to take pictures of the table.

The center pieces consisted of a beautiful arrangement of orange and white lilies bundled together with ribbons blossoming out of an elongated glass vase.

"Say cheese!" Alexia said and pulled Amanda in close with one hand as she snapped a shot of them together with the other. "Had to get one of us like we always do!"

Amanda laughed at the memory of the many times they would take a camera and snap a close shot of themselves when they got the chance. They must've had a million copies of them taking the same kind of picture in the same pose.

"This is so awesome, Amanda! It couldn't be more perfect, don't you think? We're going to remember tonight forever!"

—⁓⁓⁓—

The night wasn't as fun for Amanda as she'd hope it would be. She felt so empty without Mitch there with her.

A variety of music filled the room and the majority of the students were up on the dance floor, including Gregg and Alexia but Amanda couldn't get the drive to move from her chair.

Luca had been sitting at her side the entire time, quietly minding his own business as he looked around the room observing everything around them.

"Are you okay?" Luca finally asked as he turned his attention to Amanda.

"I guess. I'm just not in the mood when I wish I was." Amanda said as she looked over at him. "You know what I mean?"

"Well, everyone experiences hard times and nothing is easy unfortunately. I wish there was something I could do to help." Luca said and Amanda was surprised to feel his hand rest softly on her on her thigh. She knew he was just trying to comfort her but it felt strange to be touched by anyone else but Mitch.

Before she could make any type of movement, he removed his hand and stood up from his chair as Alexia and Gregg hurried over to the table once the previous song ended.

Luca was talking with Gregg while Alexia ran over to Amanda and knelt down by her chair.

"Come on! You have to get up there and dance at some point. We didn't come to prom to sulk. It's supposed to be fun, remember?" Alexia said as she tried to encourage Amanda.

"I *am* having fun!" Amanda lied.

"Liar. Come on, I know that look." Alexia said and before jumping up to her feet when she heard the next song start to play. "Oh! At least dance to this! It's easy and you don't have to do it by yourself!"

A slower paced dance song had begun as multiple couples made their way out onto the dance floor.

Perfect, a love song to dance to... without Mitch.

Amanda sighed and looked hopelessly at her friend before she spoke.

"But Mitch isn't here..." Amanda said sadly.

"May I have this dance?"

Amanda glanced up to find Luca standing beside Alexia, offering his hand to Amanda.

Amanda looked at Alexia for guidance before either accepting or rejecting his offer.

Alexia smiled and nudged her, encouraging her to take his hand.

Amanda took a deep breath before cautiously lifting her hand and placing it in his.

"I won't bite." Luca said kindly as Amanda looked up at him. "See? That wasn't so hard now, was it?"

Luca smiled as he carefully pulled her up to her feet and she followed him, hand in hand out onto the dance floor.

Couples swayed back and forth to the romantic melody that floated into the air.

Luca took Amanda's hands and placed them gingerly on his shoulders before resting his palms on her waist.

She followed his lead as they began to sway slowly to the music. Her legs felt slightly weak but her body felt awkwardly stiff and stubborn as she felt his embrace surround her.

"I hope this isn't too awkward for you. I'm just trying to help." Luca said, trying to sound as reassuring as he could.

"No, it's fine." Amanda lied. "I know I should be having a good time anyway."

"Listen, I know we barely know each other but if there's anything I can do, please let me know. I know you're hurting right now but you should really try to enjoy yourself while you're here."

Amanda looked into the blue of his eyes that reminded her of the rich blue ocean of the Jersey Shore she loved so much. Maybe getting to know someone new was a good thing after all.

"I know, thanks. I appreciate it." Amanda said shyly.

A few moments passed without either of them speaking a single word. Both of them listened to the music as they swayed back and forth, observing the couples surrounding them.

Alexia and Gregg were only a few feet away and Amanda watched as Alexia rested her head on Gregg's shoulder, holding each other close.

Amanda's heart sank a little more because all she wanted was to be held by Mitch and feel his warmth she had grown to love so much.

"Amanda," Luca said interrupting her thoughts. "I just want to say that you look stunning tonight. From what I'm told, you don't like dressing up too much, but you look absolutely beautiful."

Amanda could feel herself blush at the tremendous compliment and she found it difficult to look him in the face.

"Thank you." Amanda said then quickly decided to change the subject. "So, your real name isn't Luca, is it?"

Luca looked down at her, surprised by her question.

"Well, as a matter of fact, Luca is my nickname. My real name, my Watcher name is Lucius."

"What does it mean?" Amanda asked.

"It means light. We're the Watchers of the Earth but the good thing is that we all have different names and not just plain old Watcher. Gregg got stuck with the standard and traditional Grigori name but I got lucky. I got a name that is more significant. But how'd you assume that Luca wasn't my actual name?"

"You can only guess who told me, like she tells me everything else." Amanda said as she looked over at Alexia and his gaze followed hers.

"Ah, I see." Luca chuckled.

"I couldn't ask for a better friend. She's the best. Besides, I've kind of learned that everything isn't what it seems anymore and it's nice to have her to help me get through it all." Amanda said as Luca shifted his gaze back to her.

"Very true. It must be nice to have that kind of friendship. We, Watcher's are kind of like that. We're like brothers. We all have each other's backs."

"I'm so happy that she found Gregg. She loves him so much." Amanda said thoughtfully, admiring her friends as they danced together.

"Yes, I see that. It's nice to know that Gregg cares so much about her that he hasn't let all of this come between them."

His choice of words caught her attention.

"What do you mean?" Amanda asked curiously.

"Well, you'd figure now that everything is out in the open and she knows the truth about him, you and everything else, he'd leave her out of it so she's not put in harm's way of any kind. But he cares about her too much to let that come between them. She's fragile compared to the rest of us." Luca explained as Amanda looked back over at her best friend.

He was right once again. She had never thought about it before but it was risky keeping Alexia around.

But she couldn't bring herself to the thought of abandoning Alexia only because she knew about everything that had happened. She meant too much to her to just simply throw away the friendship they had and move on without her.

They were practically sisters. They needed each other and there was no way Amanda was going to let Alexia go on without any protection now.

"I understand." Amanda said. "But just because she's human doesn't mean anything. She's my best friend and if I know Gregg, he wouldn't have the heart to do such a thing about someone he cared about."

"Exactly my point, though. Gregg cares too much about her and he's even told me that he won't let her go. It must be nice to have those kinds of feelings toward someone; a longing to be with someone in spite of the circumstances." Luca said thoughtfully as they continued to sway to the rhythm of the music.

"It must be nice." Amanda said sadly.

"Well, haven't you felt that way before?" Luca asked confused and trying to make eye contact with her.

"I'm not sure. I thought I did but I just don't know anymore, I guess." Amanda said as she felt his hand lift and gently take hold of her chin to face him eye to eye.

"Listen, just keep your head up. Sometimes the most wonderful things can happen at the least expected moment. Just let things run their course and see what happens." Luca's words moved Amanda, making her smile.

Luca's gaze stayed fixated on hers as he slowly dropped his hand back onto her waist.

The song slowly faded into another upbeat rhythm as Alexia and Gregg came over to them.

"They can't seem to take their hands off each other." Gregg whispered loudly to Alexia for them to purposely hear.

Amanda jumped back from Luca letting go of him and almost losing her footing.

"No, we were just dancing like you told us to." Amanda said defensively.

"I believe I asked you to dance and you said yes, actually." Luca said and laughed with Gregg and Alexia.

"I think he's right." Alexia said and crossed her arms, trying to keep from bursting out with laughter.

"Whatever. We were dancing and that's it." Amanda said and blushed as she playfully punched Alexia in the arm.

The squeaking and squealing of the microphone being adjusted pierced the air as the principal grabbed it off the stand and tested it.

"Okay, everyone! It's time to announce prom court and the king and queen! Everybody should take their seats!"

Amanda, Alexia, Gregg and Luca headed back over to their table as all of the students bustled excitedly about the room.

Once they took their seats, Alexia took out her phone and quickly handed it over to Amanda.

"Here! Take pictures if I'm called up for prom court!"

Amanda prepared the phone to be camera ready as Alexia eagerly waited in her seat, hoping to hear her name come through the speakers.

One by one, student after student was called up to the dance floor as members of the prom court.

"Alexia Bellamy!" The principal called out her name as Alexia stood up, beaming with pride.

It was the moment she'd been waiting for since the beginning of high school.

"Take pictures!" Alexia said impertinently as she walked behind Amanda's chair.

"I got it, don't worry!" Amanda laughed as she started clicking the pink cell phone to death.

Gregg, Amanda and Luca watched on as the king and queen were crowned and the prom court stood at the front of the dance floor.

The next event of the prom was the king and queen's dance and Amanda set the phone down on the table figuring it was a good chance to take a break.

"You know, you should be up there. You'd stand out among all those girls." Luca said as he looked over at her.

"Standing out is the last thing I want to do right now. Thanks, anyway." Amanda said giving him a small smile.

"I'm just saying because who knows when the time will come and standing out will probably be the best idea there is. You're special." Luca said with kindness in his eyes.

He had good intentions and she knew that but she just wasn't sure how to handle it.

Learn how to take a compliment…

"I get that a lot." Amanda said as she shifted uncomfortably in her chair.

"I'm just saying, you're beautiful and you shouldn't be afraid to stand out. That's all."

Luca winked at her before looking away back at the dance floor.

Amanda blushed and looked over at Gregg to see his reaction from the comment made by Luca but Gregg was distracted. She followed his gaze leading up to Alexia at the front of the room as she exuberated nothing but happiness.

Amanda could see his love for her in the way he looked at her from across the room.

It was that unyielding sense of dedication and unconditional love filling the space around him.

Amanda looked out at the dance floor and could just envision she and Mitch dancing together, holding each other as they swayed to the music. She imagined his sweet, intoxicating scent filling the room and being held in his warm embrace as they both playfully made fun of the prom and all the silly excitement about it. She could see Mitch in a black tuxedo and possibly a deep red tie to match her gown. They would smile, laugh and he'd kiss her gently as he'd done so passionately before.

Amanda sighed as her reverie faded back into the crowded room of the prom.

Isn't that what Mitch felt for her?

Amanda knew she had loved him but had he truly loved her back at all?

Chapter 17

H⊕PELESS

The night went on and there was still no word from Mitch.

The prom was ending and students were piling into their rides to go to the post prom party. Amanda, Alexia, Gregg and Luca waited outside for their limo to pull up around the circle in front of the mansion.

"So, what do you think, Amanda? You want to come with us to post prom? It's going to be a good time." Gregg asked as he swung his arm around Alexia pulling her close.

"You should go with us! It'll be fun!" Alexia said excitedly.

Amanda stood next to Luca and she could feel his gaze watching her carefully. Amanda noticed that he had made it a point to stay by her side for the remainder of the night.

"I don't know." Amanda said unsure whether or not if it was a good idea.

"It might get your mind off things." Luca said but Amanda couldn't resist the urge to go home and wait for Mitch to show up at her doorstep.

"I think I'm going to go home. I'm really tired." Amanda said and it was the truth. She really was tired and she also wanted to be alone for a while.

"Oh, fine." Alexia said disappointingly. "But if you need anything, anything at all, please don't hesitate and just call me."

"I will. Thanks."

Once the white limo pulled up front, they piled into the car one by one. Luca sat right beside Amanda and she appreciated his company but she couldn't help but feel awkward and out of place with him.

Mitch should've been sitting there next to her.

As the limo drove off down the long road, Amanda watched the beautifully lit mansion disappear behind the trees as they headed back to Middleton.

Amanda watched her house come into view as the limo parked outside in the street. Amanda scooted across the limo toward the door as the limo driver came around and opened the door for her.

"We'll see you later. Just don't forget to call if you need anything." Alexia said before Amanda could leave.

"I will. Have fun guys!" Amanda said and stepped outside. She was walking up the steps the porch when she heard footsteps coming up behind her.

"Are you sure you're going to be alright?"

Amanda turned around to find Luca standing before her with a sincere expression on his face.

"I'll be fine." Amanda said softly.

"Please don't hesitate to reach out to me or any of us. I'm..." He stopped before correcting himself. "We're here for you."

He appeared genuinely worried and Amanda wondered why he seemed so concerned.

"I know. Thanks." Amanda couldn't come up with anything else to say.

"You really do look beautiful tonight. I... I mean that."

The Luca she had met was kind but this seemed a little overboard and his words came out stumbling one after the other as if he was nervous.

Amanda looked up at him wondering why he was acting so overly generous and even a slight bit protective.

"Thank you, Luca. But really, I'll be okay. Go have a good time tonight."

"Are you sure you don't want company?" Luca asked softly and Amanda could strongly sense that he didn't want to leave her alone.

"No, it's okay." Amanda said and looked up at him to find his wide blue eyes looking down at her.

But before either of them could say another word, Alexia yelled out from the limo.

"Come on, Luca! Let's go! The party if waiting! She'll be fine!"

Luca looked from Amanda to the limo, as if he were torn.

"Okay. Well, have a good night, Amanda." Luca finally said before turning and sprinting back to the limo.

Amanda watched the limo drive away and couldn't help but think about how odd Luca's behavior had suddenly changed during the span of the night from when she had initially met him.

Amanda shrugged it off as she walked inside the house to find Nan sitting on the couch reading her book with Oreo in her lap.

When she noticed her granddaughter walk into the foyer, Nan marked her page and placed her book down beside her.

"So, how was the prom?"

"It was... fun." Amanda said as she started pulling some bobby pins out of her hair.

"Wasn't there some sort of party afterwards?" Nan asked. "Aren't you going out with your friends?"

"Yes, there's a party but I'm exhausted. I want to go to bed."

"I don't blame you, sweetheart. I think rest is exactly what you need after such a long day. Are you alright?"

"I'll be fine. I mean there isn't much I can do, right? I just need to think about things and wait until he calls or texts me." Amanda said sadly. "And I really hope he does."

"I hope so too, darling. I'm sure he will reach out to you when the time is right."

The elderly woman picked her book back up and opened to the spot where she had left off.

"Yep." Amanda said even though she knew that waiting for him would be nothing but torture. "Goodnight, Nan."

"Goodnight, Angel."

Amanda walked up the stairs and she heard Oreo hop down off the couch and romp up the stairs, following Amanda as she headed to her room.

"Come on, boy."

Amanda signaled Oreo into her room before shutting the door and walking over to her dresser to check her phone.

Nothing.

Amanda carelessly dropped her phone onto the dresser before plopping onto her bed and with her head in her hands.

Was he really going to leave her in the dark like that?

Hopelessness was the only thing she could feel. She was numb to the world because her world had died. He wasn't there.

Would he even try to contact her?

Amanda cuddled up under her covers with the only piece of normal that she ever had, Oreo. She could care less if she went to sleep, still in her dress and face still covered with makeup.

She didn't care. Nothing mattered. She just wanted to fall asleep and never wake up.

Chapter 18

THE DREAM

fter an abundance of tears that dampened her pillow, Amanda had managed to fall into a deep sleep.

But it was anything but peaceful.

A vision from above, as if she were hovering over some sort of dark and deserted vast barren. Through the darkness she could see the dry and dusty ground tinted a dark red as if she were on the surface of Mars. It was quiet and eerie as her vision looked all around her but there was nothing and no one to be seen.

Familiar sounds arouse from the darkness as she slowly made her way in the direction in which it was coming from.

Fear overwhelmed her as she moved forward and the one thing she knew too well appeared before her out of the darkness.

The river of blood.

She stumbled backwards for fear of plunging into the rapids once again like she had so many times before.

Suddenly, she lost her footing and tripped backwards anticipating she would land on the hard ground but instead, she found herself falling through the darkness.

Her vision was lost in the abyss when she suddenly opened her eyes and to find her vision was blurred.

Amanda realized that she was tied up, strung up on either side by her hands and the unusual ropes stung anytime she tried to make any movement. She was extremely weak and she could suddenly feel burning sensations birthing from all over her body. She could feel deep lashes marking her entire body and she wanted to scream out in pain.

Amanda could make out figures, creatures surrounding her and speaking to her but she could barely make out a word they were saying.

The sound of hissing could be heard at the end of everything they said as she was beginning to come out of what felt like being unconscious.

She had been physically beaten and battered to death.

It's so real...

Her head felt extremely heavy and it reminded her of when Ravish had knocked her out cold.

Amanda managed to sway her vision to the side in an attempt to try and get a glimpse of what was tightly stringing her up by her wrists.

When her vision gave way to some clarity, she realized that her hands weren't her hands at all.

Despite feeling weak, she managed to flex her muscles in an attempt to move but found crimson claws at the end of her arms move at her command.

Where am I? What am I?

Her soul seemed to be inside some sort of creature, somehow latched onto this alien body as if it were her own.

Razor sharp thorns dug into the wrists of her clawed appendages as a dark liquid spilled down the limbs of the creature.

She could feel herself wince in anguish as the thorns dug into the creatures flesh.

Amanda could feel its desperate aching and unimaginable distress and it made her sick to her stomach. She could sense the creature's spirit trying to hold onto hers as if she were some sort of savior from deep within. The overpowering sense of hopelessness frightened her to the very bone as she felt the creatures eyes dampen with saturation.

It was crying and there wasn't anything Amanda could do to help it.

Amanda's heart sank when she noticed a significant feature that stood out to her. Fear took hold of her entire soul as her eyes grew wide with the fear of only hoping she was wrong.

The creature was missing a single digit on its hand.

In that same moment, she understood that the creature had been trying to show her what was happening as it cried out in agony. It cried out loudly from the depths of the darkness before she awoke to hear one simple word, one significant name echoing in her mind.

Amanda!

She sat straight up to find herself back in her bed, sweating and breathing heavily in shock.

Amanda could still feel the creatures fear rushing through her veins, causing her heart to pound with urgency.

It was Mitch.

He was trying to communicate with her.

Malicious.

She recalled the memory when he had explained to her that Demons could communicate through dreams.

Create nightmares.

When Demons were on Earth, they were deceivingly different in appearance. He had said their true image was not for the light hearted.

Red claws.

Her heart pounded increasingly harder against her ribs as she tried to catch her breath before bursting with tears.

Mitch never meant to leave her all alone. He would have been there.

But at some point, he had been dragged down and was being tortured in the most frightening place that she had only seen bits and pieces of in her dreams.

His home.

The Underworld.

Chapter 19

PANIC

*A*manda had no idea what time it was but she needed to figure out what she was going to do.

The sun hadn't yet breached the horizon and all she knew was that it was Sunday morning.

What was she going to do?

Amanda was sitting up in bed as she contemplated what to do or where to go. Her first instinct was to run to Mitch but she had not a clue how to find him or reach him.

She felt stuck, almost just as helpless as she had felt in her dream. The lost sense of hope made her heart ache and made her stomach quiver with nausea.

Amanda held her head in her hands as she tried to think.

Focus.

The first thought that came to her mind was the field.

The clearing.

She quickly jumped out of bed, still in her red prom dress and smudged make up that had run down her face during the night.

Oreo watched from the foot of the bed as Amanda tripped over her own feet as she quickly slipped on her sneakers. He stayed put as she ran out of her bedroom and down the hallway without a second glance.

She didn't care if Nan was awake or asleep; she just had to get to the field.

After racing across Middleton, Amanda pulled her car on the side of the road just outside town.

The daylight was starting to reach across the sky as the sun dawned from the east.

She hopped out of the car and ran toward the center of the clearing where they would always spend time together. The morning air was humid and warm as she sprinted through the tall grass.

Amanda's pace slowed as she approached what appeared to be a dark circular crater in the ground ahead of her.

As Amanda knelt down, she could still smell a lingering scent as if the area had been set ablaze and the earth beneath her feet had been scorched.

What happened?

As Amanda inspected the landscape, she tripped over an intriguing and unusual rock. But when she bent down to pick it up, she realized it wasn't a rock at all.

It was a phone; Mitch's phone.

The phone had been smoldered into a small molten piece of metal and plastic.

She looked around for any other sign of Mitch but his cell phone was all she found.

Tears started to run down her cheeks and she tried not to collapse completely.

Panic slowly crept through her as a relentless accumulation of questions started to form in her mind.

Had everyone been right? If they had been more careful, maybe this wouldn't have happened? What could they have done to prevent this? Had they really been too irresponsible and reckless? How could she find him? Who could help her? What could she do to save him?

It was difficult to leave the last place where he had last stood but Amanda managed to force herself to walk back toward her car.

Amanda took a deep breath and wiped her face as she tried to steady her tears. She glanced down at the charred cluster of plastic of what used to be Mitch's phone in the palm of her hand.

She *needed* to find him.

Amanda climbed into her car and shut the door as she plugged the keys into the ignition.

There could be one person who could help her save him.

The only person who had saved her once and maybe there was a chance that she could save *him* this time instead.

Nan.

Chapter 20

⊕NLY H⊕PE

manda raced back home to find Nan sitting on the front porch in her wooden rocking chair with Oreo in her lap.

"What on earth?" Nan asked, baffled by her granddaughter's disheveled appearance as Amanda made her way up the steps.

"I need your help." Amanda said, feeling significantly weak and out of breath. Her cheeks were still damp from her ongoing tears. It had felt as if she'd been crying forever.

"My dear, you're a mess. What's wrong and where did you go so early in the morning?" Nan asked as stood up and she placed Oreo at her feet.

"He's... gone." Amanda said as she outstretched her palm, displaying the rock of what used to be Mitch's phone.

Nan took the chunk out of Amanda's hand and observed it carefully.

"What is this?"

"It's his phone. Someone took him. He tried to show me in my dream."

Nan looked from the rock in her hand back at Amanda. Amanda stood there, makeup smeared across her cheeks, eyes pink and puffy and her prom dress all wrinkled. Nan noticed she was also wearing her sneakers as if she had run out in a hurry.

"Okay. We'll figure this out. Let's go inside, honey."

Nan wrapped her arms around Amanda for comfort as they walked inside the house, followed in by Oreo.

—⌘—

"So, he used you in a nightmare to show you what happened?" Nan asked.

Amanda nodded her head as they sat side by side on the couch in the living room.

"I don't know the whole story but he's being tortured, Nan. Practically to death and I need to find him. It was dark and there were other creatures there, torturing him. He was bleeding and in a lot of pain. I didn't even know someone could feel that kind of pain." Amanda explained. "Nan, I love him. He never meant to ditch me during prom. Something happened and he's down there somewhere. I just need to get to him."

Nan looked away, lost in deep thought and her brow creasing with a serious expression on her face without saying a single word.

"If you're asking me to help you get down into the Underworld, I'm afraid I can't do that, Amanda." Nan finally said.

"Then how?" Amanda said letting her arms fall to her sides hopelessly. "How can I find him? He needs me. He needs help."

"I'm not sure if there is anything that I can do." Nan said beside her granddaughter as she watched Amanda suddenly stand up from the couch.

Amanda stomped her foot with frustration and she could feel her anger boiling up with each second they sat there while she knew Mitch was suffering.

"There has to be something! I don't know the whole story, it's true but I need him! I need to save him! I need your help! He's dying, Nan!" Amanda said and begged her grandmother as she fell to her knees and her head rested on Nan's lap.

Nan softly stroked her granddaughter's long hair as Amanda quietly wept.

"I am an Angel, an Ancient Angel, sweetheart. There is only so much I can do. And besides, who knows what Belial has planned if he finds out you're down there."

"Who's Belial?" Amanda asked.

"It's another name that the Angels have for Lucifer or Mephistopheles."

"Oh." Amanda said and dug her head into Nan's morning robe.

"Listen to me, going down there is not safe and I'd be breaking the rules. Angels don't trespass where they aren't supposed to dwell or be."

"Who cares about the rules!" Amanda said through her tears.

"You would say that, wouldn't you?" Nan smiled. "Amanda, it's very dangerous for anyone who doesn't belong down there in the first place. Mitch is from the Underworld, he would understand."

"But he needs me or else he wouldn't have shown me in my dream." Amanda said as Nan rested her palms beneath her face and lifted her head to see her eye to eye.

"However, we should not give up on faith."

"How can you say that when you won't help me?" Amanda said as she sniffled.

"Because there is only one other person who could possibly help you with this situation."

"Who?"

"A Demon that left us long ago." Nan said to find her granddaughter looking back at her with a look of pure confusion.

"A Demon who gave me something important with very specific instructions in case she ever needs him in a dire situation. And I think this is pretty dire and important to you. Am I right?"

"Yes, but who?" Amanda asked as she looked suspiciously at her grandmother and waited for her answer.

"Your father."

Chapter 21

HIDDEN MEANINGS

"My father?!"

Amanda asked a little too loudly and stood up and backed away from Nan. She couldn't believe what her grandmother was saying.

"But I haven't even really met him before. Why would he help me now?"

"Years ago, going back to the day that they decided to part ways and go into hiding in order to protect you, your father gave me something with very specific instructions. I'm not going to promise that he will help you but it's worth a try and it wouldn't hurt to ask. I'll be right back, sweetheart." Nan said and went up the stairs to retrieve what she had been talking about.

Amanda sat back down on the couch, still in her wrinkled dress but she didn't care.

Her... father?

After all these years, her grandmother was telling her that there had been a way to contact her father.

Amanda couldn't even comprehend the concept as she held her head up with one hand on the arm of the couch.

She was just an infant when her father and her mother had left them. She had a vague memory in her mind of her mother but she had no idea what her father looked like, let alone his actual name.

Was Nan right?

Because he was a Demon, maybe he could help her after all. Maybe he could bring her to Mitch.

The reality of the situation was beginning to hit her all at once.

Was she even ready to speak with her father? Was she even ready to see him? Would he help her? Was there a chance she could meet her mother too?

What would she even say to him?

The creaking from the steps in the foyer interrupted her rapidly flowing thoughts as Nan made her way down the stairs.

The elderly woman walked into the living room with a small yellow gold box in her hand. It appeared as if it were holding some sort of ring or piece of jewelry inside.

Nan sat beside Amanda on the couch and offered the box to her granddaughter.

Amanda was hesitant at first but slid the box into her palm, unsure whether or not to open it right at that moment.

But what was in it?

Amanda opened up the lid slowly to find a very unique looking pendant that appeared to be attached to a yellow golden linked chain.

The pendant was all gold but tinted with a rose glimmer. The golden metal was in the shape of an oval and thin strands came up from the bottom as if roots were wrapped around the base of the pendant. They flowed up into what appeared as the trunk of a tree and then burst out into branches that clung to the sides of the rim.

What stood out the most were the glistening red crystals that clung to the branches as if they were a beautiful form of leaves.

The pendant was hypnotizing and flawlessly gorgeous as the two of them looked at it glowing in the box.

"You're father told me that it's one of a kind. It was made especially made for you by someone only he knows.

"Wow, it's beautiful."

"It matches your dress, Amanda." Nan said thoughtfully, noting the coincidence.

"It does." Amanda said as she unhinged the chain from the boxed and held the necklace in her hand when she noticed a small piece of paper sticking out from the bottom of the box.

Amanda slid out the paper from the small crevice on the side to find it folded in half. Before she could unfold it, Nan lay her hand on Amanda's to get her attention.

"Now, there are particular instructions with this, according to your father so listen carefully."

"Okay, what do I do?" Amanda asked, beginning to feel anxious.

"He told me that the golden metal and the enchanted red stones give you a special ability. He specifically said that when you need him, to place the necklace under your pillow at night and say the words scripted on the paper you have in your hand before you fall asleep."

Nan lifted her hand away and Amanda unfolded it to find a phrase written neatly on the inside.

Bring me to the darkest of my past, hidden in the shadows. Bring me to thy father, the eighth, my true and only blood.

Amanda read the unusual writing carefully before looking back at the pendant. She took a deep breath and looked over at her grandmother.

"I don't know if I'm ready for this." Amanda said with as much honesty as she could muster.

"It's alright, Angel. Take some time to think before jumping into something you are not ready for."

Amanda knew she needed to get to Mitch as soon as she could; there wasn't any time to waste.

"I'll do it tonight. Mitch needs me." Amanda said and stood up, ready to run upstairs. "But first, I have to tell Alexia, Gregg and Luca about what's going on. I'm going out for a bit and I'll be back later."

"Alright, sweetie." Nan said as she watched Amanda head to the foyer. "I think it might be best to change your outfit first."

"Oh, don't worry, that's the first thing I'm going to do. I think I'm done with dressing up for a while. Nothing but bad things have been happening ever since I've put this dress on."

Chapter 22

A BR⊕KΕN V⊕W

*A*manda slid out of her prom dress and took a soothing hot shower before changing into a t-shirt and capri jeans.

It was as if she felt closer to Mitch by simply letting the hot water run down her entire body. The warmth of the water engulfing her body felt so refreshing yet simultaneously, it made her heart ache to think of the last memory she had in her mind.

That terrifying dream…

As she slipped her sneakers on, she grabbed her phone and dialed Alexia's phone number from her contact list.

——◦◦◦◦——

"Wait, what?!"

Alexia sat in disbelief across the table from Amanda.

Amanda had raced over to Romano's to meet with Alexia, Gregg and Luca.

She knew that she had to tell her friends about Mitch and what her plans were.

"He's down there and I need to go find him. He could be dying." Amanda said leaning forward to try and keep the conversation private.

"Are you sure it's safe?" Luca asked, sounding deeply concerned.

"Well, that's supposedly where my…" Amanda hesitated, "…dad comes into play. According to Nan, he should be able to help me find Mitch."

The term 'dad' felt so strange and foreign coming out of her mouth but what else was she supposed to call him?

When Amanda thought twice about it, she realized she didn't even know her father's real name.

"But this is crazy! You've never even met your dad before. Do you really think he's going to help you find him?" Alexia asked before Gregg interrupted her.

"What if Mitch is where he's supposed to be? I mean, he does belong there after all." Gregg said and crossed his arms.

Amanda frowned and looked directly into Gregg's eyes from across the table.

"If he wasn't in any sort of trouble, he wouldn't have reached out to me. You have no idea what kind of pain he is going through.

They are torturing him. I know you don't like him and all but he doesn't deserve to be treated like that. He has good in him, maybe even some form of light, and regardless if you see it or not, I do and that's all that matters. Even though he has helped me with my darker side, he has done more for me than you'll ever know." Amanda took a breath before continuing. "Gregg, you're like my brother and I need your support and not your criticism. Please, just understand that I am going to find him and bring him back. He needs me and I need all of your support."

Gregg stubbornly looked away and pursed his lips together as he gazed out the window of the pizzeria in deep thought.

"Don't you guys understand? I have to do this and I wanted to tell you what happened before I just got up and left. I need to find him." Amanda said and looked from Alexia to Luca waiting for their response.

"I understand. I just wish I could go with you! Please come get us as soon as you get back, okay? I can't lose my best friend but I know why you have to go. I know how much he means to you." Alexia said as she reached across the table and held Amanda's hand.

They both looked at Luca who displayed nothing but pure concern across his face.

"I completely understand and I wish we could go with you to protect you but as Watchers, we cannot cross that line. We have no right to go down there and I don't even think it's possible. We belong here and that's where we stay. Please be safe, Amanda. I really wish you didn't have to do this, it's just too dangerous. Please be careful." Luca said as he looked at Amanda with genuine concern seeping through those piercing blue eyes.

Amanda smiled as they all turned back to Gregg who continued to stare out the window without an answer.

"Gregg, talk to Amanda!" Alexia said and nudged her big stubborn boyfriend.

Gregg sighed and looked back at Amanda, arms still crossed.

"Fine. Go. There's nothing we can do to change your mind and you've made that very clear. I understand why you're doing this and I'd do the same if I were in your shoes. It kills me to know that we can't be there to protect you. That's what I was originally here for, remember?"

"I know and I'm sorry, but I have to do this. Thank you for understanding. It means a lot to me." Amanda said and smiled with much appreciation. Amanda knew getting Gregg's support wasn't going to be easy but he appeared to see what she was going through.

"You have to understand that you're breaking my vow between your mother and I. Listen, I can't be there for you if you go and that was my job given to me by an Angel; your mother. It's very hard for me to accept this because in all honesty, I can't. It's my duty to protect you and keep you safe; to watch over you."

"I understand. But it's my choice, not yours so nothing will happen to you right?" Amanda asked.

"I'm not sure because I've never broken a vow before and this is a different kind of situation. But go, just please be careful. This could be a life threatening situation for you or anyone else for that matter and who knows what could happen." Gregg explained as his gaze narrowed in on her, reinforcing the seriousness of the situation.

"I understand. I'll be back, I promise. And I will be as careful as I can."

Chapter 23

ACE

*L*ater that evening, Amanda stood in front of her dresser looking at herself in the mirror.

What she was about to do would change her life entirely and the thought of the decision she was making made her nervous.

Amanda opened her right hand to find the pendant resting on her palm with the chain intertwined between her fingers. The pendant still seemed to give off a dim glow and it made her wonder what power it could be capable of.

Time continued to tick on and she knew that each and every minute was an excruciating moment where Mitch was being painfully abused. But she couldn't quite bring herself to fall asleep just yet. She was conflicted with the decision to face the one person who she had yet to meet.

Her father.

What would she say?

The thought of confronting him for the first time made her stomach uneasy. It was nerve wrecking to even think about meeting the man, or Demon, who left her so many years ago without having the chance to even meet him or talk to him.

This would be that first time and she was feeling extremely anxious.

Did she even want to talk to him?

Amanda couldn't pin down the exact emotions she was feeling. Mitch was so important to her and she was willing to do anything and everything it took to get him back. Even confront someone from her past despite feeling unsure about it.

She opened her right hand that held the tiny piece of paper with the mysterious saying that was inscribed on it.

Just get it over with...

Amanda closed her eyes and tried to focus on what was most important.

Mitch needs you. Do what you have to.

Amanda took a deep breath and opened her eyes before getting into bed and pulling the covers up to her chest.

She lifted her pillow and carefully placed the pendant underneath.

As she lay down, she pulled out the piece of paper and slowly read aloud the words that she was instructed to say.

"Bring me to the darkest of my past, hidden in the shadows. Bring me to thy father, the eighth, my true and only blood."

Amanda lay very still and looked around as if she were anxiously waiting for something to happen.

How could she fall right to sleep with the knowledge of closing her eyes and meeting her father?

Amanda closed her eyes and tried to relax and within moments, she could feel herself dozing off.

The truth of the matter was that she was exhausted and she knew her body needed to rest because of the events over the past few days.

She could only hope that Mitch wouldn't snag her and bring her away and into the nightmare once again.

As sleep started to take her away from her bedroom, she could feel herself relax and let go.

Ultimately, she didn't have a choice whether or not if she was ready to meet her father.

She had to do it, not only for herself, but for Mitch. He was after all, the only one who could help her save the love of her life.

—⚬⚬⚬—

Hours into the night, Amanda fell into a deep and peaceful sleep.

She dreamt of nothing until she suddenly found herself in what appeared to be a large underground tunnel of some sort.

The air was so dank and humid that she could feel her clothes already sticking to her body.

Ahead of her, the tunnel walls faded into the darkness, leading the way into nothing but black abyss. The faint sound of water droplets could be heard somewhere in the distance and it echoed throughout the dark passageway. She noticed that her feet were submersed in murky water up to her ankles and she found her hand clenching onto something tightly.

The pendant had managed to follow her into the dream as if it refused to be left behind.

Amanda took the glowing necklace and gently slid it over her head and around her neck to be sure that she wouldn't lose it.

Amanda decided to trudge forward and tried to stay as quiet as she could as she waited for any sign of life to arise out of the darkness.

Amanda froze in place when she suddenly noticed a change happening to the pendant. Its glow seemed to be increasingly throbbing, growing brighter and brighter and she also could sense that she was no longer alone in the shadows.

She looked around but couldn't see much of anything but the murky water at her feet and the tunnel walls on either side of her.

But she knew she wasn't alone. She could feel it.

Her senses were telling her that something or someone was behind her.

Amanda could feel fear building up within her but for fear of what exactly, she wasn't sure.

The fear of the darkness? The fear of meeting someone she wasn't expecting? The fear of confronting her father?

Amanda turned around cautiously not knowing what to expect. She held her breath when she saw a figure standing at least twenty feet away from her.

She squinted through the dark to try and make out what the person looked like but all she could make out was a singular silhouette of what appeared to be a tall and well-built man. She tried to look more closely and could make out that he was a middle aged man.

He didn't move and he didn't speak. He simply stood there watching her.

"Who are you?"

It was the first and only question she thought of to ask but when there wasn't any response, she didn't know what to do or say next.

Amanda mustered up some courage and decided to try and get closer to the person. She went to walk forward when the man raised an arm, signaling her to stop.

"Don't. Stay where you are." The mysterious man warned.

When Amanda heard the sound of his low voice, she realized he had a distinctive English accent.

"Why?" Amanda asked but obeyed his command. "Who are you?"

"It's been years…" The man said with a sad tone as his arm descended back to his side.

"Did… did you give me this?" Amanda asked nervously as she lifted the glowing pendant away from her chest.

The man remained unmoved as if he didn't know how to respond.

"Did you give me this?" Amanda repeated.

"Yes."

Amanda didn't know what to say but all she knew was that her father was standing before her for the first time.

"Dad?" Amanda asked as the word came off her tongue as if it were some form of foreign language she had spoken.

It sounded so strange…

"Yes, Amanda. It's me."

She didn't know whether she wanted to run to him and hug him or stay as far away from him as she could. Her heart felt torn as she tried to grasp the reality of what she was experiencing.

"I can't see you, can you come closer?" Amanda asked, curious to see her father for the first time even though she was unsure about everything she was doing.

"I can't. It's better to stay in the dark. It's hard to explain." Her father said and remained motionless. "Amanda, I am so..." he hesitated, "...sorry."

He was definitely a Demon. She could hear the pain behind his voice when he forced the word out for her to hear. She knew it all too well from all of her experience with Mitch.

Amanda couldn't say it everything was okay because it wasn't. For years, she had been longing to meet her father and even when the truth had been finally revealed, neither of her parents came out from hiding to help her. She barely knew him but she wanted to kick and scream like a small child, upset and angry at him for leaving her without even checking in once.

Despite what her grandmother had explained to her and their reasoning for their actions, it still hurt her.

What could she say?

"Nan told me I could find you with this." Amanda said and gestured to the pendant as it fumbled between her fingers as it sat around her neck. The moment was so awkward she didn't really know what to do or say. "Well, here we are. I have so many questions. I mean, I don't even know your name."

"Ace. You can call me Ace."

"Ace." Amanda repeated to herself.

It was an unusual name for a Demon. She wondered if it had any significance similar to that of Mitch's.

"I, well..." Amanda struggled to find the words, but decided to get right to the point. "...I need your help."

"There's only so much I can do for you and I can't make any promises."

His choice of words instantly offended her having not even known her request.

If there was only so much that he could do, why would he offer his help to begin with?

"Of course you can't keep promises, you're a Demon." Amanda said before realizing how bitter the words sounded. "I'm sorry, I just, I had no one else to turn to and this is, well, it's..."

"It's hard, I understand. What is it that you need? What can I do to help you?"

"Someone I care about has been taken and I can't get to where he is without your help. He is a Demon, like you."

A moment of silence rested upon them both before Ace spoke.

"Where is he?"

"He's in the Underworld and he'll die if I don't get him out. Please, help me?" Amanda begged and she started to feel tears forming behind her eyes. The memory of Mitch's nightmare refused to leave her mind forcing her to push forward and do anything to get him back.

Ace sighed as if he were struggling to say something.

"I can't." Ace said finally as he looked away from Amanda.

"Why? I've never asked you for one thing my entire life and you say you can't help me with this one thing?" Amanda said as tears broke free from her eyes and spilled down her cheeks.

"It's complicated." Ace said.

"Please? Please!" Amanda pleaded desperately as she felt panic beginning to overcome her. He was her only hope and if he refused to help her, she didn't know what she would do. "Why can't you do this to me? I need you for the first time in my life and you can't be here for me? I love him! Do you hear me? *I love him!*"

Amanda felt her legs weaken and she fell to her knees, causing the water to splash all over her but she didn't care. She held her head in her hands as she sobbed uncontrollably.

Ace looked back at his daughter appearing to be conflicted with the situation. After a few moments of considering his daughters request, he took a step forward and spoke.

"Okay. I will take you there." Ace said with sympathy. "Please, I can't stand to see you cry."

Amanda wiped her face and looked up at her father's silhouette.

"You'll help me?" Amanda asked through her tears.

"Yes, but you have to listen to me very carefully."

Amanda slowly got back on her feet, feeling her heart rise with hope.

"What do I do?" Amanda asked.

"When you awake, I need you to go to a specific location as soon as possible. Look at the note that came with your necklace, it will say where to go. Meet me there and remember to be discreet."

"But all it had on it were those words I said before I fell asleep." Amanda said, confused.

"Look again. Trust me. What you need will be there."

Amanda looked at him, perplexed by his demand. She was convinced that she hadn't seen anything else on the tiny piece of paper.

"Okay."

"Are you sure you want to do this?" Ace asked his daughter as if he wanted her to reconsider her decision.

"Yes, I need to."

Amanda couldn't understand why he was being so stubborn.

Why was it so hard to take her to the Underworld? He was a Demon, wasn't he? He could easily bring her there, right?

Ace nodded and turned to leave without a single word.

"Wait!" Amanda said. "Where are you going?"

Ace stopped and seemed to look over his shoulder before disappearing into the darkness of the tunnel.

"To the portal. You better be on your way." Ace said before vanishing into the darkness ahead of her.

Chapter 24

MORE THAN MEETS THE EYE

*A*manda awoke to find the morning sun peeking in through her window.

She quickly lifted her pillow to find the pendant still lying where she had placed it. She placed the necklace around her neck and held the pendant in her hand.

For the first time, she had spoken to her father and she sat quietly for a moment in disbelief. The pendant actually worked and took her directly to him in her dream. It felt so strange to have talked to him without actually seeing him.

Ace…

It was an unusual name for a Demon and she didn't get the chance to ask what it might've meant.

The memory of the environment she had dreamt of lingered in her mind. The dark tunneled passageway and the water at her feet made her wonder if they had been in an actual location somewhere and not just out of the imagination like a dream typically was.

Why would he have picked such a dark place for her to meet him for the first time?

Amanda remembered him mentioning the piece of paper and she scrambled around her bed in search of it.

When she found it on the floor beside her bed, she thought that it must've managed to fallen as she had slept.

The front side of the small paper read nothing but the phrase she had been instructed speak in order to see Ace. She flipped the paper over to find new writing centered on the back. He must've somehow placed it on during the course of the night.

Inscribed were only numbers with a single letter at the end of each grouping:

44° 31'30.17"N 110° 50'17.48"W

It took her a moment to think about what they could've meant before her eyes widened when she recognized them as coordinates.

They seemed to be coordinates pointing to a very specific location.

Amanda sprung up from her bed and slid into her chair sitting at her desk as she opened her laptop.

Amanda pulled up a search engine and typed the numbers carefully into the search bar and pressed enter.

The first thing that came up on the screen was an image of a small map with an arrow pointing directly into a lake.

Amanda retyped the coordinates once more to make sure there wasn't any mistake but the same exact thing popped up on the screen.

A lake?

Amanda clicked on the image to expand the map across her screen to find that the lake was located in Yellowstone National Park in Wyoming.

The lake was called The Grand Prismatic Spring.

She clicked on a website that described the lake in hopes of getting some more information.

Some excerpts described it as a massive boiling lake, as hot as one hundred and sixty degrees Fahrenheit. It was as wide as three hundred feet and one hundred and sixty feet in depth. The location was once designated as Hell's Half Acre which immediately caught Amanda's attention. There was definitely some sort of actual relation to the reference and Amanda instinctively knew it.

According to all of the sites she browsed through there had been multiple scientific evidence and history that explained why the volcanic geyser was the way it was but Amanda knew better. If her father was taking her there, to some sort of portal that he had mentioned, there was more to it than what could be studied by any scientist or geologist.

Amanda moved the mouse arrow over to the images tab on the top of the screen and typed in the name of the spring.

The screen was flooded with very interesting, almost alien like pictures of what appeared to be the spring. The spring was a beautiful multitude of colors spanning from the beautiful orange and yellow rim to its rich green and deep cerulean blue center. The term 'prismatic' seemed to fit the description perfectly with its beauty and variety of colors.

It most definitely appeared to be something supernatural, almost too beautiful to imagine that it would exist on Earth. She knew and had learned about Yellowstone from her geography class in school but didn't realize something like this belonged within the park.

It was beyond breath taking, even through the computer screen with its unique beauty.

Amanda leaned back in her chair and wondered what it would be like to see it in person.

Why did Ace want her to meet him there?

She remembered him mentioning something about a portal before he vanished from her dream. He had also said to be discreet.

What did he mean?

Amanda got up and wondered downstairs in search of Nan. She rounded the corner to find Nan sitting in the living room with a book in her hands and Oreo in her lap.

"Did it work?" Nan asked curiously as she closed her book.

"It did but he wants me to meet him somewhere. He gave me coordinates." Amanda said as she took a seat beside her grandmother.

"Hmm, so, this means he is going to help you after all?"

"Well, he gave me a hard time about it at first but eventually said that he would."

"I thought so."

"But why would he not help me? I mean, I've never asked him for anything in my entire life."

"Well," Nan paused and thought before answering Amanda, "what you're asking for is nothing short of a small task, it's a big favor. He has his reasons and he is after all, a Demon. Besides you, more than anyone else should know how stubborn they can be. So, why wouldn't he give you a hard time?" Nan said and smiled.

"I know but I just figured he'd be more open. I guess I just expected something without thinking about how he'd feel about it. I don't know. I'd just expect he'd be there for me no matter what, but I guess I should know better because of what I've already been through."

"True, but remember that they did everything they did for you. It wasn't because they necessarily wanted to leave you alone. Remember our talks?" Nan asked as she wrapped her arm around her granddaughters' shoulders.

"Yes, I know." Amanda said before changing the subject. "He told me to be discreet. What do you think he meant?"

"Well, he provided you with coordinates which seems to me that he couldn't blatantly tell you where to meet him. It's as if he had to use some other code, some other way to tell you. Did you find out where these coordinates tell you to go?"

"It's in Yellowstone National Park at some lake or spring." Amanda said as she played with the pendant around her neck.

"I see. This is across the country which means you'd have to fly." Nan said and Amanda looked at her grandmother with excitement in her eyes. "But, I think he wants you to actually fly in a plane, not fly, fly."

"Oh, come on! I've been wanting to fly and practice that more! This would be perfect!" Amanda said, practically begging her grandmother.

"No, no. I think this has to be kept as a secret. He probably wants you to act normal and not do anything out of the ordinary. I think it's for your own safety, that's probably why."

"Oh, fine!" Amanda said and sighed with disappointment.

"When did he tell you to meet with him?" Nan asked.

"He said as soon as possible."

"Well, you better go upstairs and look up some flight tickets. You have a long trip ahead of you."

Chapter 25

FAREWELL

Once Amanda booked her one way flight to Jackson Hole Airport in Wyoming, she started stuffing her back pack with a day or two worth of clothes and the daily essentials that she wasn't even sure she would need.

Amanda had called Alexia and asked if her best friend would be willing to drive her to the Newark Airport just over an hour away. Alexia was more than happy to oblige and she was due to arrive at any moment.

The flight was due to depart in just a few hours and Amanda felt as if she had no idea where she was going to end up. She had never flown on an airplane before, and there she was, prepared to take a chance and fly all alone.

She decided to change into a pair of dark jeans and a red tee-shirt with her usual pair of sneakers. The occasion wasn't going to be anything fancy other than meeting her father for the first time so she decided that casual was the best way to go.

Amanda grabbed her MP3 player and headphones from her desk and slid them into the front pocket of the backpack. With a six hour direct flight into Yellowstone, she knew her MP3 player would be the best thing to occupy her mind on the plane.

She took a glance around the room to make sure she had everything she needed.

The pendant was strung around her neck, resting on her chest and it caught her eye in the reflection of her mirror before she left the room. It made her think about the dream and the only image she had in her memory of her father.

The dark silhouette in the shadows who claimed he was her father. It was the only thing she had and she was incredibly anxious to finally see him in person.

As Amanda shut her bedroom door behind her, she heard Alexia enter the foyer downstairs and greeted Nan.

"Hi, Nan!" Alexia said and peered up the stairs before quietly starting a conversation. "Are you sure this is a good idea? I mean, does she know what she's getting into?"

Amanda stopped before rounding the corner to head down the stairs as she tried to listen to the hushed conversation.

"I think she knows what she's doing. She's been given instructions by her father and she just has to be careful. This is what she wants." Nan explained.

"Okay, I'm just worried. I don't want anything bad to happen. She barely knows her dad and I know she loves Mitch but I was talking to Gregg and Luca last night and they're really worried."

"Have faith, Alexia. Even though Amanda is stubborn, she is smart. There is nothing else that we can do right now but pray that she stays safe."

Amanda knew that her grandmother and her friends were worried but she needed to go. Nan was right about her being so stubborn but her mind was set.

She needed to save Mitch somehow.

Amanda decided to make her way down the stairs and found then standing by the front door together.

"Hey! You ready?" Alexia asked as she placed her hands on her hips.

"Yep. Everything's all set." Amanda said stopping before them.

"Okay, then let's go!" Alexia said and walked out the front door toward her car.

"Amanda, please be careful. I love you very much." Nan said stopping Amanda before she could walk out the door.

"I will. I promise. I love you too." Amanda said and hugged her grandmother tightly.

It felt as if she were saying goodbye and never coming back. It felt so strange to be leaving all on her own and unsure of where she'd end up. All she knew was that she was going to see her father and get Mitch back.

Before Amanda walked out the door, Nan displayed a smile at her but Amanda could sense that it was forced and more of a nervous smile than anything else. She knew her grandmother was worried but there was no going back now that she found her first connection to one of her parents and there was a possibility to rescue her boyfriend, her Demon, Mitch.

The drive up the Garden State Parkway to the airport consisted of oddly nothing but quiet.

Amanda knew that her friend was worried and probably didn't know what to say. There was nothing she or anyone could do or say to stop her from going.

Only music played softly from the cars radio as they drove in silence.

Amanda looked over at her friend who appeared calm and collected but she knew Alexia was anything but.

As Alexia drove onto the ramp for the exit toward the airport, she turned the music off.

"Well, we're here." Alexia finally said.

They drove around the expansive circle in front of the airport toward the appropriate terminal drop off point.

Alexia pulled over, close to the entrance and turned to Amanda after coming to a stop.

"Amanda, I know you've heard this a thousand times already, but I'm worried for you." Alexia said with genuine concern.

"I know. I'm worried too, but I have to do this. Mitch needs me."

"I know he does. Just, please, come back to us no matter what. You're my best friend and I can't lose the only person who is practically a sister to me. Gregg and Luca wish they could go with you." Alexia explained having realized the reality of the situation and the possibilities of what could happen. "We've been through too much to lose it all."

Amanda leaned in and hugged her friend tightly from across the center console of the car. Alexia was the most wonderful friend anyone could ever have and Amanda knew how lucky she was to have her in her life.

"You won't lose me. I'll be back. I promise."

Amanda knew that she couldn't actually keep any of the promises she was making but she was determined to come back no matter what happened. The only difference is that she would only come back with Mitch by her side and she was going to stop at nothing to make that happen.

Amanda pulled away and looked her friend in the eyes before getting out of the car.

"I'll find Mitch. I know I will. Like Nan says, have faith. At this point, I think that's all we have."

Chapter 26

HIGHWAY T⊕ HELL

*A*manda plopped down in her coach seat next to the window after getting her ticket and going through the security check point.

She wasn't looking forward to the long flight and the thought of being so far away from the only place she'd ever been made her stomach feel queasy.

Amanda fastened her seatbelt and looked out the small oval window to find the wing of the plane directly below her, spanning out across the tarmac.

She thought about her friends and her grandmother, about how worried they were for her. She truly wondered what she could've been getting into.

She took a deep breath and then reached into the front pocket of her backpack to pull out her MP3 player.

Music seemed to be the best thing she had in mind to ease her nerves.

After she slid her tiny buds into her ears, she placed her backpack securely beneath the seat in front of her.

As the plane started to roll away from the terminal, the stewardesses walked down the aisle, performing the routine security check demonstrations.

Amanda turned the MP3 player on and as she listened to the first track play from where it left off, she looked inquisitively at the device.

She immediately recognized the song playing loudly into her ears as Highway to Hell by ACDC.

Mitch.

He must've been listening to the song the last time he had stolen her MP3 player.

Ironic.

Amanda sighed as she tried to make the decision whether or not it bothered or comforted her.

She finally decided to let it play on as she closed her eyes and forced herself to drift off into a nap.

Amanda had a long day ahead of her and she knew it.

The faint sound of a man's voice on the flight's intercom system brought Amanda out of her sleep. She opened her eyes and yawned to find that she had somehow shut off her MP3 player as she had squirmed in her seat. She pulled out her ear buds as she peered out the plane window to find that they had landed at the Jackson Hole Airport in Wyoming.

The weather was clear and sunny and the sky was a beautiful pristine blue. There were massive snow topped mountains in the distance and nothing about the scenery reminded her of New Jersey at all. She was far away from home and all on her own.

Once all of the passengers made their way out of the plane, Amanda tried to navigate her way through the airport, following signs for the exit. The building almost reminded her of a log cabin with the wooden ceiling and its structure.

Before she had left the house, she had looked up and written down a phone number for a cab company to pick her up at Jackson Hole. She was too young to rent a car and it's not like she was familiar with anyone from Wyoming to pick her up and bring her where she needed to go.

Amanda slid a small piece of lined paper from her pocket and pulled out her cell phone and dialed the number she had scribbled on it.

The time was four o'clock and it would be minutes until they could pick her up so she decided to go outside and wait, rather than wonder around in the airport.

She stepped outside to find the air a little cooler than it was back at home. Despite the fact that it was summer, she assumed the altitude of the land is what caused the weather to be a little cooler than what she expected.

She took a moment once she walked out the glass doors to admire the unique landscape. It was vast and beautiful, displaying a completely different side of the country.

Amanda dropped her backpack down beside one of the pillars, next to a garbage can as she sat down on the concrete and waited as patiently as she could for the cab to arrive.

The airport had an interesting design with wooden pillars along the glass walls of the front of the building beneath a large wooden awning.

Amanda played with the pendant around her neck and pulled it forward to admire its beauty once again. As she looked at it, she could only think of how it resembled the likes of her father.

Amanda wasn't sure exactly how far the Grand Prismatic Spring was from the airport, but she knew that she'd see her father soon enough and the thought made her nervous.

She knew that he would help her find Mitch and that was exactly what she wanted. But in the back of her mind, she was hoping he'd be willing to stay with her and possibly come home with her too.

Would he help her and then just get up and leave her once again?

Either way, she knew she was doing the right thing. Mitch called upon her for help.

He needed her and every moment she was away, he was hurting. Every moment that passed, he was dying.

For all she knew, he might not even still be alive but she needed to find him.

Amanda anxiously tapped her foot on the ground as she grew more and more impatient when she heard her stomach growl.

She was hungry.

Amanda looked around and found a vending machine not too far away from her. She tried to regain her focus and conjured up a dollar from out of the pocket of her jeans.

As she slid the dollar into the machine, she browsed through the different candies and bags of chips before finally deciding to pick a package of peanut butter cups.

After she grabbed the candy, Amanda sat back down next to her backpack and opened the snack.

Amanda knew it wasn't going to fill her up but it was her only option. She couldn't remember the last time she had eaten and that last thing she wanted was to start feeling sick to her stomach between not eating and nervously awaiting the confrontation.

As she ate the candy, she glanced up to see the cab pulling up along the curb.

Amanda jumped to her feet, swung her backpack over her shoulder and tossed the wrapper into the garbage can as she walked over to the car.

She opened the back seat door and slid into the cab.

"Yellowstone National Park?" The young cab driver asked peering at her through the rear view mirror.

The kid looked as if he were in college taking up a summer job as a cab driver or something of the sort.

"Yes, please. Can you take me to the Grand Prismatic Spring?" Amanda asked.

"Well, I can take you to the main gate. Once you pay admission, I'm afraid you're on your own." The cab driver said as they pulled away from the curb and headed down the road toward a main highway. Signs read that they were going toward a highway called US-191 North and as Amanda looked around at her surroundings, she really had no idea where she was. She needed someone to take her to exactly where she needed to be.

"But I need to get to the spring somehow." Amanda said as she tried to think of a way to get to the spring without flying or getting lost. She had no idea where she was or how to get to the place where her father told her to go.

As Amanda gazed out the window a thought crossed her mind and she looked at the driver through his reflection in the mirror.

"Well, what if I paid for your ticket too and you could drive me there once we're in the park?" Amanda asked, knowing that she could just conjure up the money from her hands without having to worry about the cost.

"Oh, I don't know, mam..." The kid said sounding unsure as he weighed his options and contemplated on taking her offer.

"Well, do you have to pick anyone else up because if you don't, then you could have a free day in Yellowstone? You know, a fun day exploring the park?" Amanda insisted. "I mean who wouldn't want a free day to do whatever they wanted to at Yellowstone?"

"Well, no, I don't have anything else scheduled..." The young man said as they continued to drive.

"It'd be fun, besides I really need to get there and it would really help me out." Amanda said and smiled as she borrowed one of Alexia's batting-of-the-eyes techniques. "Please?"

The young man looked from the road to Amanda then back to the road as he debated on accepting the generous offer.

"Oh, alright. It'd be kind of neat to spend the day there. I haven't actually gotten the chance to visit other than drop people off or take people to a hotel in the area. I have to make sure my boss doesn't find out. Are you sure?"

"I am more than sure! And no one will ever know, I promise. It's my pleasure, just as long as you take me to the Grand Prismatic

Spring." Amanda said smiling as she leaned back into the seat and watched out the window.

"Okay, then. Grand Prismatic Spring it is!" The driver said as they drove onward.

"How far away are we?" Amanda asked as she admired the mountains and hills along the horizon.

"About two hours or so."

Chapter 27

DESCENT

"Well, this is the closest I can drop you off." The driver said as the car slowly rounded the small cul-de-sac in the parking lot. The cab came to a stop where there appeared to be a path entrance. "You'll have to take that path over there to get to the spring, I think."

"Are you sure this is it?" Amanda asked as she looked around through the window.

"That's what the sign said. Do you need to be picked up later?" The kid asked and looked at her from over the seat.

"No, it's alright. Someone is meeting me here and well, I'm sure they'll give me a ride. I just needed someone to get me here." Amanda said and reached into her pocket for more cash. "Here you go."

Amanda reached over the seat and handed the kid some more money before grabbing her backpack and slinging it over her shoulder.

"Thanks, again." Amanda said before sliding across the seat and stepping out of the cab.

The car pulled away, leaving her alone at the end of the road with no choice but to head down the path toward the spring.

The first thing Amanda noticed was a terrible odor lingering in the air that she could barely tolerate.

Amanda sighed and tried to ignore the smell as she looked around for a moment, trying to take in her surroundings.

The parking lot was practically empty and she appeared to be the only visitor entering the path toward the spring. The thought of being so alone and in a place she'd never been before, made her want to fly back home.

But she had gotten this far and she wasn't going to turn back. She could only hope that Mitch was still alive.

The sky was still a gorgeous blue and there were a few large trees lining the parking lot and around the end of the road. She turned to face the direction where the path led and saw clouds of steam rising from the earth in the distance.

The steam only made her think of Mitch whenever the rain would land on his heated skin but she knew that it was only steam rising from the hot spots and geysers in the area.

Amanda recalled the interesting information she had learned in her geography class at school about the unique park as she started to make her way down the dirt path.

The vast national park was home to Wyoming, Montana and Idaho, consisting of many canyons, rivers, and mountain ranges.

After all, Yellowstone was one of the most beautiful places in North America but also one of the largest super volcanoes in the world, waiting many years to erupt at any given time.

With each step she took, she could feel her heart pounding with anticipation and the unusual sensation of fear in the back of her mind.

She was alone, in a place she was unfamiliar with and about to confront someone she always wanted to meet but wasn't sure that she could trust entirely.

As she continued onward around a wide bend, boardwalk-like planks replaced the dirt as she noticed the ground was getting increasingly damp, hot and steamy.

Amanda rounded the corner and saw that the pathway formed into a bridge leading over a river bank of hot water coming from what she assumed to be the geysers. The bridge didn't have any rails and it made Amanda all the more nervous to cross the platform. A small sign before the bridge read the name of the flowing river as Firehole River.

It appeared to be like any other river with grass and trees lining the edges except for the clouds of steaming rising from some locations along the river's sides.

The place was already beginning to be somewhat familiar to her.

The heat, the steam, the fire reference…

Amanda decided to keep moving down the path as steam grew increasingly thicker as she made her way across the bridge.

The next sight along the path was the Excelsior Geyser which could barely be seen through all of the steam hovering above it in the air.

Through breaks in the steam, it didn't appear to be erupting or spouting any water into the air like Amanda had expected but instead seemed to be a large but calm and peaceful lake.

Amanda continued onward, passing a vast wet area that appeared to reflect the blue sky. There were brown veins of soil spreading throughout the ground creating a unique mirrored mural of the sky above it.

With each and every passing, Amanda could see why Yellowstone was so greatly admired for its beauty and interesting landscape even though she had only been exploring one small location out of the entire park.

After sightseeing multiple hot springs along the path, she walked through the thick steam and toward what she expected would be her final destination.

The Grand Prismatic Spring.

As Amanda approached the spring, she looked around in search of her father but no one could be found

The steam seemed to clear up slightly, enabling Amanda to see some of the bright colors contained inside the spring.

The bright red-orange lining of the spring became clearer as she got closer with each step she took down the path.

Yellow, green and blue peeked through the steam and it seemed to lift higher as Amanda took in the breathtaking sight.

The pictures that she saw online had been taken from above, displaying all the colors in full effect. However, in person and despite the steam rising into the air, the colors were still vibrant and intense.

The prismatic wonder had to have been longer and wider than a football field and its mesmerizing colors alone defined the explanation for its intriguing name.

The large center was an electric, cerulean blue, practically resembling the color of the ocean in any isolated island paradise.

Amanda dropped her backpack onto the path and stood in awe of the striking wonder of a lake when she suddenly felt as if she were not alone like she had in her dream.

"Hello, Amanda."

The voice came from behind her and she instantly recognized his voice.

She turned around to find him, her father standing a few feet away from her.

He was tall; at least just over six feet high with short brown hair and familiar hollow black eyes.

The only difference she noticed about his eyes was the sad look about them and he had a five o'clock shadow. He looked slightly disheveled as if he hadn't slept in days even though she knew very well that Demons didn't sleep to begin with.

"Hi…"

Amanda couldn't bring the term 'dad' out from her tongue; it just didn't feel right just yet.

"You can call me Ace, for now. I know this is hard for you."

"Okay, umm, Ace." Amanda said awkwardly. "Why did you bring me here?

"Behind you is an entry way, a portal, if you will, to the Underworld."

Amanda looked behind her at the Grand Prismatic Spring before turning back to her father.

"That?" Amanda asked and pointed behind her.

"Yes. It was once known as Hell's Half Acre. There are other areas of this park with names that provide hints to what lies beneath this very Earth, this innocent world." Ace explained.

"What other names?" Amanda asked curiously, but still keeping her feet planted where they were. She refused to get too close to him because he was still a stranger in her mind and in her heart.

"There are many other places within this magnificent park known as The Devil's Den, The Devil's Well, The Devil's Hoof. As you can see, there is a reason why they are named this way. Yellowstone is not what it seems." Ace said and pointed in the direction of the spring.

"But why is it so... colorful? It's so beautiful. I'd think Hell wouldn't have such a pretty portal I guess." Amanda said as she turned to observe the spring once more.

It was hypnotizing and unique.

"Well, humans and scientists have been studying this entire park for many years. This is the largest hot spring in the country. They believe that because of the different species of microorganisms and bacteria in the water and when they are combined with the volcanic rock and the boiling temperatures of the ground from beneath, they say it causes the color combination that you see. But you and I know differently. There's a whole significant amount more to it than any ordinary person could know." Ace explained.

"What do you mean?" Amanda asked.

"It's anything but an average science experiment of organisms and heat. The Lord," Ace winced in pain before explaining and Amanda understood the move entirely too well. "Well, White light is what protects the Underworld from joining this world. It keeps it in its rightful place; it's a boundary that cannot be crossed."

Amanda looked at him with an inquisitive expression.

"In other words, when the sun's light hits the White Light that rests upon this place, it causes this supernatural effect, this blend of colors that you see as beautiful. It's an invisible barrier that prevents the Underworld from going anywhere except where it's supposed to stay. So, when humans say that it looks alien or as if it just looks as if it were from another world, it really is but no one knows the truth except supernaturals, like Demons and… Angels."

"Wow." Amanda looked at the bright colors amid the thin layer of steam rising into the air. "So, that barrier can never be broken?"

"Well, there is one thing that can break it, but I'll explain later." Ace said. "This is one entry way into the Underworld."

"There are other ways? Like, other portals?" Amanda asked intrigued and eager to find more answers to her many questions.

"Yes, there are portals all over this world. From Pluto's Gate in Turkey to Hekla, the volcano in Iceland."

"So, why are we going through this one?" Amanda asked.

"This one is not used as often and it takes us to a spot that isn't as open as the others. It's like a back door to the Underworld but we still need to be as quiet and careful as we can."

"I understand." Amanda said before Ace abruptly cut her off.

"Amanda, are you sure you want to do this? It is, above all, dangerous, and not only for you, but for me as well." Ace said and hesitated as if he had said something amiss.

"Why do you keep asking me that? He needs me and I need to find him before it's too late. Nothing will stop me from getting to him."

Amanda couldn't help but read worry all over his face and in the tone of his voice. She had a funny feeling that something was wrong and he was too afraid to explain why he kept asking her the same question over and over again.

Ace looked at her for a few moments, seemingly admiring every detail of her face.

"You really are as stubborn as I thought you'd be." Ace said thoughtfully as the corners of his mouth tipped up into a slight grin before becoming serious once again. "Okay, we will go. Just understand that the Underworld is a place of everlasting destruction and darkness. A place of hopelessness and suffering. Nothing can prepare you for what you're about to see."

Amanda swallowed hard as she started to realize how serious her journey to find Mitch was going to be.

"I... I understand." Amanda found herself stuttering nervously but there weren't any other options.

"You cannot be weak. I know you are strong and you need to stay that way, alright?" Ace said.

"I'm strong, believe me. I can do this." Amanda said despite her mouth becoming increasingly dry.

Ace walked past her toward the spring as Amanda leaned down and picked up her backpack, preparing to leave when she heard Ace speak.

"I don't think you'll need that where we're going." Ace said over his shoulder and chuckled.

Amanda stood there dumbfounded and watched him walk away as he signaled her to follow.

She dropped the backpack on the path and sprinted ahead to catch up to him.

Amanda followed him until he stopped along the path and turned to face the spring.

"Now, you have to trust me. Are you ready?" Ace asked while his eyes stayed transfixed on otherworldly spring.

Amanda took a deep breath and tried to relax her tense body.

"Yes, I'm ready. Let's go." Amanda said as she felt her father's hand gently take hers into his.

"Don't let go of my hand." Ace said and even though it felt odd to feel his touch for the first time, she held on as tightly as she could and in a flash, they had jumped high into the air together.

Amanda tried to look around but before she could get a glimpse of how high they really were, she felt her stomach drop as they started to fall fast through the air.

She looked down to see the colors of the spring rapidly approaching from beneath them and the air was growing hotter and hotter as they quickly descended downward.

Amanda closed her eyes tightly for fear of hitting the boiling spring below.

She only thought of Mitch and gathered every ounce of courage she had before plunging down into the dark world of the unknown.

—◦◦◦—

Falling...

The sensation reminded her of falling out of the rollercoaster when Ravish had tried to kill her.

The memory almost made her panic but she tried her best to stay calm knowing that she wasn't alone.

Amanda hadn't known how long they had been falling but she still managed to have a tight hold with Ace's hand.

Her hair was whipping all around her and it made it hard to see anything around them.

The air was still immensely hot and humid, almost making it hard for her to breathe.

As they continued to fall, she managed to look up and see the Grand Prismatic Spring far above them but only it was the opposite side, the bottom side from underneath. They had jumped through the spring into what Ace called a portal and they both didn't get burned in any way whatsoever.

It seemed to be getting darker and darker as they continued to fall faster and faster.

"We're going to hit soon." Ace yelled at her but she could barely hear him.

"What? What do you mean?" Amanda yelled back to him but it was hard to hear with the air wafting loudly against her ears.

But before he could answer her, she felt her body hit a hard, hot surface. They had both hit the solid bottom with such great force that without even knowing it, she was knocked unconscious.

Chapter 28

THE UNDERWORLD

The heat radiated from the dirt surface that Amanda could feel pressing against her body as she lay motionless on the ground.

Amanda had no idea how long she had been lying there but the heat seemed to bring her out of her lethargic state.

Something or someone was nudging her side as if they were trying to awaken her.

Amanda rolled over onto her back and she felt as if her entire body had been bruised.

As she forced herself to sit up, she opened her eyes and tried to keep herself from falling over from her dizzying vision.

Before she could look around her, she held her head in her hands to try and steady her sight and ease the pain throbbing throughout her body.

"Are you alright?" A voice asked her.

Amanda instantly recognized Ace's voice except that had a raspy and deeper tone he normally sounded.

"How long was I out for?" Amanda asked refusing to look up just yet.

"I'm not sure."

Amanda looked down at the ground and once her vision gained some clarity, she saw that the ground beneath her was some shade of crimson. She ran her fingers along the unique looking dirt to find it dry and dusty, as if she were in an alien desert or on the face of Mars.

"Did… did we make it?" Amanda asked as she observed the red dust along her fingers.

"Yes. We landed a little harder than I expected but yes." Ace said.

Amanda went to stand up when she stumbled backward at the shocking sight of her father.

He no longer looked like the man she had met, but instead his appearance had completely transformed into a hideous looking creature.

The dim environment surrounding them made her feel even more alone with him, with this monster and it terrified her. Amanda was surprised that she didn't scream at the first sight of him however it had scared her right off of her feet and she fell once again onto the hard ground.

His entire skeletal structure had altered into a very tall, boney monster. Ace's skin color was dark red, like that of a garnet, from the top of his hairless skull down to his black hooves of what used to be his human feet.

She saw that his knees were inverted, like that of a bird or some sort of unique creature.

His eyes were similar like before, entirely consumed with darkness and his ears were pointed upward and away from his head.

His teeth were sharp and jagged making him appear all the more threatening and ferocious.

A Demon.

"It's alright, Amanda. It's still me. Don't be afraid." Ace said softly and crouched down beside his daughter.

She heard his voice and despite the slight change, she found it difficult to believe that the creature was truly him.

The only physical features she recognized were his sad, dark eyes. He had a melancholy aura about him and it showed in both of his forms and she wondered why he always sounded so down and out.

She had just met him, and barely had a chance to get to know him before seeing him as this beast. From the shadows of a dream to meeting him in person, it all blew her mind away.

Was this all really happening?

"I know I'm not the prettiest thing to look at, but this is how I am. This is… the real me." Ace said sadly, as if he were ashamed of his very existence.

So much for introductions…

Amanda recalled the memory of Mitch explaining to her that his true form, his Demon form, was not for the light-hearted and that she wouldn't want to see what he truly looked like.

Amanda finally understood what he meant but it got her curious and she couldn't help but think about the nightmare she had when Mitch made contact with her for help.

She had seen his sharp claws, red skin and dark blood spilling down his arms.

Amanda took a deep breath and tried to collect herself when she heard Ace speak.

"Don't be alarmed and I know this is a lot to take in, but you don't look quite the same way either." Ace said and backed a few feet away from her.

As Amanda got up to her feet, she looked down at herself to find that he'd been right.

She *was* different.

Amanda was significantly taller and her skin tone had a hint of a pinkish-red, as if she'd been sun burnt. She also noticed her nails were pointed, black and sharp to the touch, resembling claws.

Even the dark streaks in her long hair had taken over and blonde could no longer be seen on any strand on her head.

She hesitated before glancing down at her feet, hoping that she didn't have anything else but her normal, human toes. But when she saw that legs were similar to Aces' and her feet had been transformed into little black hooves, she felt her stomach drop.

"What? Wait, why did this happen? Ace, what happened to me?!" Amanda asked as she felt panic starting to take hold of her.

"Amanda, you are after all half Demon. You were bound to change when you got down here."

"Well, thanks for the late reminder!" Amanda said sarcastically.

She was visibly upset with her new appearance and had blatantly forgotten that it was possible for her to change. "But will I stay like this? I've never changed like this before."

Amanda peeked over her shoulder to find her wings could be seen for the first time without resting her White Light upon them.

They were large in size as she'd seen before but this time they had physically changed and her wings were dark, feathers as black as a raven's wings.

As she outstretched them with her sore muscles, she also noticed the tips of her feathered appendages faded into blood red.

Amanda also noticed that her red tee-shirt had been torn up; displaying some of her midriff and her jeans had been slightly ripped up.

She looked at Ace, not knowing what to think of the change and feeling slightly embarrassed by her more revealing appearance. She tried to pull down her shirt to cover her stomach but it was no use; the shirt was too shredded up to do anything about it.

"I think it suites you." Ace said as he took his clawed fingers and stroked his chin, observing her new look.

"Well, you would say that, wouldn't you?" Amanda said. "Now, what?"

"Well, I can't give you a tour of the Underworld." Ace said awkwardly.

"I wasn't expecting a tour anyway. You already know why we're here." Amanda said and put her hands on her hips and looked around but couldn't see much through the darkness around them. "It's so dark. Is that all that the Underworld is? Dark?"

"Darkness is one of the most feared elements of the mind. It makes you feel cold, alone and ultimately, hopeless. You never know what could be lurking in the dark. Besides, when Mephistopheles was banished down here, he made the most of what he had. His hatred for the worlds above him just grew and grew so I guess you can say it fits him. This is just a small part of it but this is his king-dom... my home."

Amanda didn't know what to say but she could sense her father's ongoing sorrow whenever he'd speak.

"You're not like any other Demon I've met before. Well, I can't say I've met a lot because I've only really met two but you seem so sad and depressed about all of this. The other Demons I've met aren't like you at all. Why are you so sad?"

"Well, I have my reasons. But don't worry about it. Let's just keep moving." Ace said uncomfortably and started to walk ahead into the darkness. "There's only one place I can think of where they might have taken him. Follow me and stay quiet."

Amanda couldn't help but feel like he didn't want to talk about something, as if he were keeping another secret from her. She kept trying to pin down why he must be so sad but it appeared that he clearly didn't want to get into a conversation having to do with himself.

As they made their way through the darkness, not a sound could be heard except for Amanda's repetitive tripping over her own hoofed feet.

"Damn it! I can barely walk with these!" Amanda said as she grew increasingly frustrated, trying to stay close to Ace.

"Shh… stay close. Getting lost in the darkness down here is… well, let's just say death is the worst case scenario."

"Oh, okay thanks. Well, now I feel better." Amanda said sarcastically.

The darkness gradually began to lift as they approached an area illuminated by large flaming torches.

"Get down." Ace said as he crouched low to the dusty earth.

Amanda obeyed his instructions and got down on her alien-like hands and knees and followed his lead.

Ace stopped at the edge of what appeared to be a cliff that cut off and dropped down into the shadows.

He stayed very still and didn't say a word, his sight transfixed into the darkness below.

"Now, what?" Amanda asked a little too loudly, as she grew more and more impatient.

"Shh… look closer." Ace said and Amanda could hear a hint of fear in his voice but she was unsure of what he was exactly afraid of.

Amanda glanced down into the darkness and noticed that the cliff didn't vanish into the shadows below them, but instead when the flames light hit the darkness, it reflected itself on a dark liquid. It was as if there was a black ocean beneath them and stretching out into the abyss beyond.

It sounded like a goopy substance, squishing and making deep bubbling sounds, as if it were a vast lake of hot, boiling tar.

"What is that?" Amanda asked, curious about the strange pool.

"It's The Obsidian." Ace said nervously and swallowed hard.

"It's the what?"

"The Obsidian. No one knows about this beast other than those who reside in the Underworld."

"Wait, it's alive? That *thing* is alive?"

"Yes."

"But it's like some kind of liquid or something. Kind of like the Blob?" Amanda asked before realizing that he probably wouldn't understand the reference.

"The Blob?" Ace asked and turned to Amanda with a curious look on his face like she suspected.

"Never mind." Amanda said and rolled her eyes.

"I don't know what the Blob is, but this is called The Obsidian. It's kind of like the Devil's secret weapon."

"A secret weapon for what?" Amanda asked even though she feared his answer.

"You won't like the answer." Ace said, seemingly reluctant to respond with the truth.

"Tell me. If it's important, then tell me."

"It's the Devil's release on to the world. It will devastate the world as we know it; in other words, the apocalypse."

Amanda took a deep breath.

"Yeah, I'd say that's pretty important."

"It's his key to break out of here. When Hell breaks loose on your world, the apocalypse will begin and this will take part in consuming and utterly destroying everything in its path. Anything that's tossed into that thing will be obliterated into nothing, not even a creatures soul can survive once they've touched that thing."

The bubbling tar boiled below them and with each massive pop of its sticky goo, it made Amanda's stomach jump.

"And this is just a part of it. It reaches way out there in this huge canyon." Ace said and pointed out into the darkness ahead of them.

"Great." Amanda said with the utmost sarcasm. "And when is this supposed to happen?"

"It's said that Mephistopheles will release it when the final battle between Heaven and Hell takes place. But no one is sure when that will be. He calls the shots and can make that choice at any time. But no one is sure why he hasn't done it already. No one knows what he's been waiting for."

Amanda had no words, she was speechless. A war between Heaven and Hell at any time simply made her sick to her stomach.

But if Mephistopheles had something so powerful, so devastating, even she wondered why he wouldn't have used it already.

What was he waiting for?

"But how can it break through the barrier of White Light?"

"Well, remember how I said that only one thing is capable of doing that? Well, this is it. It's said that Mephistopheles infused his White Light inside of it when it was created, along with the many tricks up his sleeve, which enables it to do anything, including breaking that boundary holding Hell in its place. It's like a ticking time bomb of evil waiting to explode."

"Can anything destroy it? What can stop it?" Amanda asked and turned to Ace.

"I'm afraid I don't know. No one is sure and I would assume that only Mephistopheles or the guy upstairs would have any knowledge of that."

"God would have to know, right?"

"Sadly, I'd have no way of telling."

"There's got to be a way…" Amanda said thoughtfully.

"I'm sure there is but for now, let's try to find your friend. I wanted to show you this because it could happen at any time and Earth, the world in between, is your home. I'm sure you'd want to protect it." Ace said and turned around to head in the opposite direction. "Come on, let's move on."

Amanda took a moment to think about what he had said before finally moving away from the cliff's edge to follow Ace.

The end of the world? Would it really happen?

She could see another dimly lit area in the distance and followed behind Ace as she tried to steady her footing.

Balancing on hoofs was not easy given that they were heavy and bulky.

"How do you deal with this?" Amanda asked as she took baby steps in an attempt to keep her balance. "Can't you slow down? I mean this is kind of difficult for me."

"Well, I've had mine for quite some time so it's different for me. I'm sorry; I promise I'll slow down." Ace said and waited for her to catch up to him.

"Thanks."

Once Amanda reached his side, she pointed off into the distance ahead of them.

"What's that over there?"

"I think that's where we'll find your friend. Stay close."

Chapter 29

MALICIOUS

The torches glowed brightly from below them as Ace and Amanda peeked over the edge of the cliff.

Amanda had no idea what to expect but nothing could prepare her for what she had seen in her dream and the horrible things that he was going through.

Amanda anxiously peered down below them to see exactly what she didn't want to see.

Below them were an abundance of creatures, Demons, torturing what appeared to be ghost-like glowing figures strung up by fiery chains.

With each loud crack of every whip and each anguishing cry that pierced the hot air around her, Amanda could feel her fear growing with each beating pound of her heart.

"What are they doing? What are those?" Amanda asked.

"Souls."

She could feel tears building up from behind her eyes and she could barely look on at the monstrous scene.

It was excruciating and it was as if she could feel their pain lingering in the air around her.

"Amanda, are you alright?" Ace asked having noticed Amanda's saddened expression.

"Why are they doing that? Why are they whipping them?" Amanda said and looked away.

"Those aren't ordinary whips. They are capable of ripping out each and every single quality of any soul. With each whip, it tears you apart. You slowly lose your dignity, then your will, then your love, and so on and so forth until you're then left with nothing and your soul falls to pieces. Every memory you ever loved, gone. Absolute emptiness and pain as you break down and live with nothing but their sins weighing them down for the rest of eternity. Souls are left here to exist in nothing but pain and only the everlasting memory of what they committed forever. It's nothing but misery, utter torment and anguish resulting in absolute… depression. And with each crack of every whip, their glow slowly fades away."

"My God…" Amanda said with disbelief.

Just the thought of being stripped of everything you've ever known, everything you've ever experienced had to be painful for any living soul.

"What you see down there are the souls that have committed sins and deserve punishment. If one violates God's will," Ace hesitated and closed his eyes before continuing, "they are sent here. Once you've committed a sin, you must be punished. That's just how it goes and that's the way things are. This is the way of life in Hell. It's anyone's worst nightmare and this is one reason why I didn't want to bring you down here, for you to see all of this."

"What are the other reasons? Why didn't you want to bring me down here?" Amanda asked.

"Don't worry about it." Ace said almost cutting her off mid-sentence.

She couldn't help but assume that he was possibly keeping something from her, something that he definitely didn't want her to know.

Amanda turned her attention back to the horrific scene below and then quickly turned away before she could get too sick to her stomach.

"It's horrible, I can barely stand this. Their screams are heartbreaking." Amanda said, grabbing hold of her chest as if her heart were hurting. "Whatever happened to forgiveness?"

"Forgiveness is nonexistent here. Not in this world. Once you've committed a sin and you enter through the gates of Hell, there's no turning back. I understand it's painful to watch but we are here to find your friend so let's keep moving. If I'm right, he should be in that corridor over there." Ace said and pointed down toward a little tunnel across the way.

"Let's go, I can't watch this anymore." Amanda said and back away from the ledge. "How do we get down there?"

"Follow me."

Amanda followed Ace along the edge of the cliff and saw him start to make his way down a jagged slope to the bottom.

"Try not to slip."

"Umm, that'll be impossible." Amanda said, looking down at her hooves and back up at Ace. "I hate these things."

"Here," Ace turned to face her and held out his arms as if he were offering to carry her, "it might be easier this way."

Amanda looked at him and hesitated before making the decision that he was right. It was going to be awkward but if she wanted to get down the sharp rocks without clumsily falling down them, she'd probably be better off being carried.

Amanda slipped into his embrace as he scooped her up with one arm under her knees and the other under her wings against her back.

"I got you, don't worry." Ace said reassuringly. "Here we go."

Ace carefully stepped out onto the uneven rocks, one hoof at a time as he made his way down the steep slope with Amanda in his arms.

It felt strange but in a way Amanda felt safe in his embrace. He was different, not like the Demon that she assumed and expected. He wanted to take care of her and bring her to where she needed to go and he clearly displayed exactly that. He was trying to help and she acknowledged that and was genuinely thankful for it. He didn't have to but he did.

"Thank you." Amanda said shyly but as sincerely as she could. She meant it and knew that she needed him.

Ace stopped halfway down the cliff and looked down at her and Amanda could see more than just a Demon was somewhere in the darkness of his eyes.

"Don't thank me. I'm supposed to be here for you. I care, Amanda. I want you to know that. But I had to leave you and for reasons I'd rather not say right now." Ace said and for a brief moment, the sadness in his voice was no longer there.

Amanda looked up at her father and tried to resist the urge of asking the many questions she was so eager to voice.

"But why did you do it? Why did you leave? I've always wanted to know." Amanda asked as she watched sadness creep back into his expression and the corners of his mouth turned down into a frown.

Instead of answering her, he turned his attention ahead of him and continued onward down the rocks.

Amanda simply looked up at him, disappointed once again that he was only giving her unclear answers, if any at all. She studied his interesting, demonic face with its interesting shade of red and sculpted structure.

She lifted her hand and looked at her own skin, tainted by the otherworldly blood that flowed through her veins. She was very much a part of him and his world even though she wasn't fond of it.

Once they reached the bottom, Ace leaned down and placed Amanda back on the ground.

"This way." Ace directed without stopping.

Amanda followed him along the edges of the jagged walls in the shadows before Ace stopped and turned to her.

"You go ahead and make sure to stay along the walls. I will distract them."

"But..." Amanda went to speak when Ace cut her off.

"Go!" Ace said and quickly brushed her off, pushing her into the shadows toward the direction of the dark entry way.

Ace wondered out into the open, heading toward the Demons that continued to beat and persecute the souls bounded by Hellfire.

Amanda had no choice but to move onward toward the entry way like Ace had instructed her to.

She stayed close to the wall as she stealthily made her way closer and closer to where she hoped Mitch would be. Her heart began to beat harder and harder in her chest as she moved slowly, hoping that no Demons would catch her as she did her best to remain in the shadows.

Ace seemed to casually blend in as she watched him make his way out into the open area with the other Demons.

If she had to admit it, they scared her. The Demons scared her right through to her very own soul somewhere deep within her. They were monsters that were eager for each and every soul's pain and distress. They seemed to get every ounce of pleasure in beating the souls to a lifeless pulp, leaving their glow continuing to die into nothing, just like Ace had explained.

The cries that filled the air were shrieks and they were more than ear piercing, almost so distracting that it almost restricted Amanda from moving forward.

The angelic side of her wanted to reach out and help as it instinctively had a tendency to do but Amanda knew she was helpless. There wasn't anything she could do and as Ace had said, it was the way things were down in the Underworld.

Amanda finally reached the entry way and slid, continuing to stay as close as she could to the wall.

Then she saw him.

Mitch.

She knew it was him the moment she saw him despite his demonic form because of her dream.

He was across the small cave, motionless with his head bowed as if he were lifeless, gone.

A torch on either side of him on the wall of the cave lay a blanket of soft light on his badly beaten body.

Amanda walked over, covering her mouth in shock as she felt tears run down her face and sizzle right off of her skin. It reminded her of when the rain would land on his human skin and boil up into the air, surrounding him in steam.

"Mitch..." Amanda said and hoped he would respond but he remained inanimate.

As she approached him, she saw his claws were strung up by thorny branches as they had been in her nightmare and his red skin stained with dark streaks of blood down his limbs.

She looked closer at his clawed hand to find his one digit missing and she knew it was him.

Her heart pounded harder and harder in her chest to the point where she could feel the pain but didn't care.

Amanda fell to her knees in front of him, weeping at his hoofed feet.

Was it really too late? Was he gone?

"Mitch, please. Please, don't leave me. I need you." Amanda said and attempted to touch him but couldn't bring herself to caress his lifeless body.

She felt helpless not knowing what to do to help him. All hope started to drain from her heart even though she had done everything to get to him, it was too late.

Amanda held her head in her hands and continued to cry when she heard a groan.

"Amanda..."

Mitch's voice gurgled out from his throat and she looked up hopelessly and thought that it might've been just her imagination with the last bit of hope withering away from her.

But when she saw his head swing to his side and his eyes open slightly, she knew it wasn't just her imagination.

"Mitch! You're alive!" Amanda said and jumped to her feet.

"You're... here." He managed to say before coughing up some of his dark blood.

Amanda quickly went to his hands and tried to figure out a way to get him freed from the thorns grasp but they were dug in too deep.

"Oh, God." Amanda said and wanted to cry at the sight of him. "I don't know what to do. How do I free you?"

Mitch was unresponsive and Amanda got right up and close to his face.

"Mitch! Please, wake up! I need to get you out of here! What can I do?" Amanda said as she tried not to let him hear the panic in her voice.

Amanda didn't care what he looked like in his demonic form but she knew that he never wanted her to see him like this.

Amanda took his head in her hands and tried to get his attention.

"Mitch, please. What can I do?"

Mitch's eyes rolled to the back of his head and she knew he was completely out of it and exhausted. But all that mattered was that he was alive.

She gently kissed his warm cheek and put her forehead to his.

"I will get you out of here. I promise. Please, please stay alive for me."

Even though it felt as if she were trying to comfort a complete stranger, she knew he was somewhere inside the creature before her very eyes.

Amanda backed away and tried to assess the situation and think more clearly. There had to be a way to get him out of the thorns painful grasp.

Amanda could hear a sudden commotion outside the cave and she thought of Ace. She didn't know what was going on but she had to act quickly.

"Please, just… work." She said to herself and tried to concentrate.

The only hope she had was to use her White Light and try to break the thorns hold on Mitch.

Amanda tried to conjure up any good energy, any hope that she could to project her White Light but she couldn't seem to force out anything from her hands except some white sparks that didn't do anything but disappoint.

"Come on!" Amanda yelled as her patience wore thinner and thinner. Time was of the essence and she needed her White Light now more than ever before.

"Work!"

But nothing emerged except rapidly fading white orbs that disappeared into nothing.

Amanda could feel tears forming in her eyes at the sense of regret of not having listened to Gregg.

He had been right all along.

She should have been practicing her White Light and by the time she had decided to give it a try, it was too late. It had been too long ever since she had used it last and she needed it more than anything.

There was no time and Amanda needed to get him out before they were caught.

"Amanda!"

Amanda could hear Ace yelling for her from outside the cave when he suddenly ran inside as he tried to catch his breath.

"I was only able to fight them off for so long. They will be in here at any moment. We need to leave now!"

Amanda noticed Ace freeze when he caught the sight of Mitch strung up amid the dim light.

"Malicious?" Ace asked, his eyes wide and curious.

"Do you know him?" Amanda asked.

"He is one of the Devil's most loyal hunters of The List and has been for a very long time. There was word that he broke his oath and lost his ring. He is the first hunter to refuse his responsibility of his missions. Mephistopheles must've finally got him back and dragged him down for his choices." Ace said in disbelief and looked at Amanda. Ace inspected Mitch's wounded arms as he tried to configure a way to release him. "He's who you've been talking about this entire time?"

"Yes. He did it all to protect me. I was the next one on The List and he couldn't do it, not after all we'd been through. I just didn't know better then. It was hard for me to accept everything that was happening. I don't think this would've happened if I had just stayed with him." Amanda said as tears ran down her face once again.

"I see. Okay, we need to act quick, Amanda. I don't see any other way to do this than ripping him out myself. Stand back. We have to get him out and we have to do it now." Ace said as he inspected the thorns digging into Mitch's limbs.

"What are you doing?" Amanda asked as she watched Ace reach out to grab the branches.

"What I have to." Ace said and yelled out in agonizing pain as he took hold of the branches and ripped them out, freeing Mitch one limb at a time.

Amanda cringed as she watched her father take the thorns into his clawed hands as they plunged deeply into his own skin.

Once Ace was able to free Mitch, Ace dropped to his knees, weak from the punctures in his hands.

Amanda leaned down, taking Mitch's heavy body onto her back, wrapping his arms around her chest.

He was heavy but she seemed to be having more trouble with her footing rather than the weight of his body resting on her back.

Demons were supernaturally strong and lifting Mitch didn't seem to pose as much of a problem.

Ace got back up to his feet, palms bloody and swelled with pain.

"Thank you." Amanda said and looked over at him.

"Thank me later. Let's get out of here and fast."

"No one is going anywhere." A hideous voice demanded.

Ace and Amanda froze as they watched the two Demons step into the dim light.

"Ravish. Rabid." Ace greeted them even though they were obviously unwelcome.

Amanda's stomach dropped as she watched the two Demons enter followed by an army of other Demons, completely blocking any possible way of getting out of the confined space.

"Well, well, look what we have here." Rabid said eagerly, his teeth barred as if he were hungry enough to eat them.

Rabid appeared to be like any other Demon except for the excessive amount of drool hanging from the sides of his mouth. Amanda noticed his constant uncontrollable twitching and quick movements as well as a crazed look in his dark eyes.

Rabid certainly defined his character with no questions asked.

"Try to calm yourself, Rabid; for now, anyway." Ravish said as she looked Amanda up and down. "It looks like someone's had a few changes after getting down here in the Underworld. You're a little darker than I remember. How's the new set of hooves, Amanda?"

"And you're a lot uglier than I remember." Amanda said with a snide tone as Ravish huffed at the comment.

"Feisty." Rabid snickered.

The torches light reflected against something on Ravish's hand and Amanda instantly recognized the ring.

Mitch's ring.

If there was one thing that Amanda wanted, it was to get that ring back to its rightful owner. The last place it belonged was in Ravish's grasp.

"Amanda, I don't believe you've had the opportunity to meet my other half, Rabid. We've both been waiting for your arrival. I'm glad it worked." Ravish said.

"What do you mean?" Amanda asked cautiously.

"Oh, Mitch wasn't only brought down here to be punished. You're just so naïve that you didn't expect that we'd also be waiting for you. It's as if you dragged yourself down here for us. Thanks for saving us the work."

It had been a trap all along. They knew she'd come for him but she hadn't even considered the idea.

Amanda tried to contain her anger even though she wanted to attack Ravish and tear her apart.

"But we weren't expecting *you*." Ravish said and turned her attention to Ace. "What an unusual surprise after so many years. What are you doing here anyway?"

"That's for me to know and for you never to find out. You're not going to stop us, Ravish." Ace said and got into a fighting stance, ready to attack at any moment.

Ravish definitely was nothing like Amanda remembered her. She was certainly ugly like the rest of them and no longer had the appearance of a punk-rock goddess.

"Wow, it looks like we hit the jackpot. The Sin herself... and Acedia. Wait a minute..." Ravish pointed from Ace to Amanda, as if she were trying to connect the dots. "Wow, no wonder you disappeared. I wouldn't blame you after what *you* did. This is very interesting."

Amanda looked at her father, curious as to what Ravish had been referring to.

"What did you do? What does she mean?"

Amanda waited for an explanation but he stayed silent and his gaze remained transfixed on Ravish.

"Oh? She doesn't even know who you really are? Wow, I guess I always have to be the one to spoil the surprises. It is, after all, fun so I'm not going to complain. But, poor little Amanda knows nothing about her *father*. How sweet of you to finally come out of the dark after so long just to help your little sin you've brought into the world." Ravish taunted.

"Shut it, Ravish." Ace said.

"I see that with his help, you've found your man. Too bad he's practically dead. He got what he deserved for his lack of loyalty. Too bad he's so weak; such a coward."

Amanda could feel her anger boiling over and she couldn't restrain herself any longer.

"You shut your mouth!" Amanda yelled furiously. "You don't know anything about him! He's not the weak one, you are! You have no idea how strong he is compared to you! He's stronger than you'll ever be!"

Ace looked down at Amanda, impressed with her spiteful remarks toward the wicked Demon.

"Isn't it cute when she's angry?" Ravish said to Rabid with a smirk on her monstrous face. "We'll see about that."

"We'll see about nothing." Ace corrected her. "We're leaving and there's nothing you can do about it, Ravish."

"You're not going anywhere if The Master has anything to say about it." Rabid snickered as his slimy tongue slid between his jagged teeth.

"Besides, he's been waiting for your arrival, Amanda. He's been eager to see you... again."

"Again?" Amanda asked confused.

"Oh! There I go again, almost ruining another surprise." Ravish said, covering her mouth shyly with her clawed hands. "You're coming with us and if you don't come willingly, then we'll gladly drag you. Remember how that felt, Amanda?"

Amanda took a deep breath as she tried to suppress her anger. She didn't want to play Ravish at her own game because for all she knew, it would possibly give the revengeful Demon the advantage.

Amanda cringed at the memory of being dragged down the boardwalk as she came in and out of consciousness that dreadful night in the few months before.

Amanda glanced up at Ace, looking for what she wasn't sure of but maybe some hope in his eyes except to find nothing but a sense of fear.

Realizing that there weren't any options left, Amanda got a better hold of Mitch who was still lifelessly swung over her back.

"Fine. We'll go with you."

Chapter 30

EPITOME OF EVIL

*A*manda tried to maintain her balance with Mitch swung over her as she reluctantly followed Ravish and Rabid through the darkness of the Underworld.

Ace followed closely behind as they continued to walk onward, surrounded by Demons and having no choice but to follow them into the heart of Hell.

Amanda had no idea what to expect but she was curious when Ravish had mentioned that she was going to see Mephistopheles... again.

What did she mean?

As they made their way through the eerie unknown, Amanda could make out a lit area in the distance, amid high mountainous terrain.

There seemed to be some sort of building, a silhouette of a pointed structure, resembling a castle resting between the steep ridges of red rock.

As they made their way up what appeared to be a pathway leading directly to the mysterious location, Amanda glanced around her to observe the surrounding landscape.

Beyond the high rocks and boulders, she could barely make out a horizon of mountains and random spotted areas lit by torches.

Steam rose up from dark pits in the earth and Amanda tried to repress her sense of fear as they got closer and closer to the castle.

A familiar smell crept up into her nose and she recognized it as the same unbearable scent that she smelled when she had arrived at the spring.

"Jeez, what is that?" Amanda asked as her face scrunched with disgust.

"Brimstone, or what you would know as sulfur. Remember, this world rests atop a volcano." Ace said quietly from behind her.

"It smells absolutely horrible." Amanda said, feeling her stomach churn.

"Well, we *are* in Hell. It's not going to smell like roses."

"Quiet you two!" Ravish hissed.

Amanda wanted to lash out at Ravish but she refused to put Ace, Mitch and herself in anymore danger than they already were.

Rabid seemed unpredictable and above all, threatening with his seemingly erratic behavior.

She would just have to wait until the time was right.

As they continued up the mountain, a sound could be heard and Amanda knew the sound all too well.

Her heart skipped a beat when she noticed a river flowing past them. It was dark and bubbling hot, right out of Amanda's nightmares.

The river of blood.

Amanda swallowed hard as if she could imagine its metallic taste in her mouth once again. Her stomach grew weaker at the thought of fighting against the rapids and trying to gasp for air amid its thick flow. As they walked past it, Amanda's urge of wanting nothing more than to get out of there was at its ultimate peak.

They rounded a corner to find the large building before them and Amanda realized that it wasn't a castle at all.

It was a church.

But it was the opposite of what any ordinary church would be. It was a stark black church with sharp, pointed spires and steps leading up to a set of intricately designed doors.

A large circular, stained glass window was centered high in the front with an image that appeared to be some sort of crown surrounded by falling feathers.

Amanda recalled the memory of the stories told by her grandmother as she'd been growing up.

The stories said that Satan was originally known as Lucifer which had multiple meanings referring to the shining star, morning star or son of the morning, who was an Angel of Heaven before his fall from grace.

Lucifer, an exalted Angel created by the Lord himself, considered himself a favorite among the other Angels but his perspective drastically changed when the Lord created his son, Jesus Christ.

The Lord ordained that Christ was equal to himself that wherever he may go, the Lord would be also present. Christ would carry out his will and his purposes.

However, Lucifer insisted that he be treated and be told the secrets of the Lord's will as well, just as he had entrusted unto his son and would be fulfilled by him.

But when the Lord refused and ensured that only Jesus would know of his secrets and mysteries, Lucifer became envious and jealous thus beginning a rebellion against his creator.

God had commanded unquestionable obedience by the Angels, including Lucifer, but Lucifer expressed nothing but his contempt and selfishness against the Lord, rebelling against God's will.

It disrupted the order of Heaven, resulting in a war within Heaven itself.

The Angels tried to convince Lucifer that because of the existence of Christ and the blessings that were given to him didn't detract Lucifer's significance but he refused to believe them.

The Lord then cast out Lucifer for his selfish and hateful acts, thus transforming the Angel into what was considered the Devil, or Satan along with his followers and any and all of his sympathizers.

To go against God's will and God's judgment was the highest of crimes and Angel's wept the loss of their fellow companions but God's will was done and peace in Heaven was then resolved.

Hell was then birthed and that was where the fate of Lucifer, or Satan was to dwell forever more.

The ruler of the Underworld.

The stories made her wonder if the fallen Angel, Lucifer, was just beyond the large doors standing before them.

For years, she had been unknowingly raised by an Ancient Angel and told many stories of the faith but until she had learned the truth, she had always been unsure of what she should've believed in.

And there, before her very eyes, beheld one of the key elements she could remember from the stories.

Ravish took hold of the large wooden handles and forced them wide open, revealing the inside of the sinister cathedral.

This was the heart of Hell.

An ear piercing screech could be heard from the rusted hinges of the doors as it echoed in the space around them.

Amanda's eyes followed the vast arches that reached high up into the cathedral, disappearing into the mysterious darkness above them.

Torches were lit throughout the basilica and anything that the light didn't touch was eaten away by the shadows.

Ace and Amanda followed Rabid and Ravish down the eerie aisle as they passed the rotting pews wrapped in jagged, thorny vines, row after row.

The smell of decay was so strong that it she could barely stand it.

Lined along the walls, Amanda noticed large, black cloaked figures lingering in the darks, staggered along the walls on either side of them. She couldn't make out if they were statues or real live figures when she suddenly recognized exactly what they were.

Amanda remembered the visions she had been having over the previous weeks. They were the same strange figures that were haunting her wherever she went and they were now right before her eyes. They all stood very still as they seemingly watched them walk down the aisle.

Amanda swallowed hard and tried to hide any sign of fear that could possibly be seen.

As they continued onward, Amanda felt her hoof land in a pool of something sticky on the rocky ground. She lifted her leg to find that she had stepped in a small puddle of goopy, hot blood but before she could do anything about it, a Demon from behind her forced her to keep moving.

Amanda's eyes followed up the aisle to the head of the church as she dreaded what was waiting in the darkness ahead of them.

When they finally reached the last pew, Rabid and Ravish stopped as if they were waiting for something.

"Well, well, well. So, we meet again, Amanda."

The deep voice rumbled out of the darkness before them as Amanda looked closer and noticed a large silhouette that seemed to be sitting on a throne of some sort.

It was Lucifer.

Amanda's muscles tensed and she prepared herself to stand her ground. There wasn't any way that she would let him get to her even though she had no idea what to expect. All she knew were the stories that had been told to her for so many years.

And there he was, right in front of her.

But before Amanda could ask what he meant, Ace took a step forward and spoke.

"Mephistopheles, it's not her that you want. It's me. Leave her be." Ace said abruptly.

"Acedia, how nice of you to come back. A sacrifice that you've made all because of your dear, sweet Sin that you've committed."

"What does he mean?" Amanda asked as she turned to Ace, expecting an answer but received nothing but a mournful sigh.

"Interesting... Looks like there's a lot of explaining to do..."

The voice said from the shadows and they all watched as the creature rose up from the throne and slowly stepped out into the dim light.

Amanda couldn't believe her eyes at the sight that she saw standing right before her.

The creature was the epitome of hideous and pure evil. The monster had vast scaly wings and jagged horns jutting out from the top of his skull.

His eyes bright red as if they were burning and he could incinerate anything with a single glance.

To Amanda's surprise, he wasn't as powerful looking as Amanda had expected. Instead, he appeared elderly and fragile but his presence remained ultimately threatening and intimidating.

His wings seemed to be falling apart, as if decay had long been eating them away, leaving behind patches of old flesh and skin so thin that it looked almost see through.

The monster's teeth were sharp and large, almost too big for his mouth and steam blew out from his nostrils as if he were a colossal dragon.

"You look like you're surprised, Amanda. Don't you remember me?" Mephistopheles asked curiously.

"What are you talking about? I think I'd remember if we'd met before, and you look like someone who'd be hard to forget."

"Oh, come on now. Don't be so naïve. I don't look at all familiar?"

Amanda was unmoved and she wasn't going to let him toy with her.

"I'd bet you'd remember me like this?"

A blast of red dust engulfed him and when it fell back onto the ground, Amanda didn't want to believe what she saw.

"I bet you remember me now, don't you?"

The massive creature had turned into a tall, bald man with an all too familiar pair of ice blue eyes.

"You're, you're, you're..." Amanda found herself stuttering with shock.

"That sexy red dress was perfect, wasn't it?"

"Don't you dare talk to my daughter that way!" Ace yelled and went to lunge forward when Demons grabbed him and held him back from behind.

She had truly met him before but had no way of telling. It angered her to have known that Alexia was right there with her, talking to the real and actual Devil.

Amanda's stomach dropped as she watched Mephistopheles signal another Demon to come forward and stand beside him.

"I'm sure you'll remember my lovely assistant, Lily? Or as I'd like to call her, Lilith."

The Demon transformed into the slender blonde woman in the black mini dress.

Amanda couldn't speak and her knees grew weaker until she fell to the ground.

She wanted to cry knowing that it had all been a set up.

Suddenly, before Amanda could speak, a group of Demons grabbed hold of Mitch and tried to pull him away from her.

"No! Don't touch him!" Amanda said, refusing to let go of Mitch.

Demons came from behind her and pulled her away from him, causing her to lose her grip as he slid out beneath her fingers.

"No! Don't touch him! Don't hurt him!"

"Isn't this sweet? And after all she's been through just to get him back. Pity." Ravish said as she stepped beside Lily.

"Shut it, Ravish!" Ace yelled as he struggled to get loose from the creatures holding him back.

"Acedia, I wouldn't say another word if I were you." Lilith said snidely.

"Lilith, sweetheart, would you please take Acedia and Malicious out of here? Amanda and I need to have a chat."

"Yes, Master." Lilith obeyed.

Mephistopheles signaled the other Demons to drop Amanda as she fell to her knees.

"And take Ravish and Rabid as well. You know where to go." Mephistopheles said as he watched them make their way back down the aisle.

"Where are you taking them?" Amanda asked but didn't receive an answer.

"Amanda! Don't listen to him! Whatever you do, don't take the bait!" Ace yelled before the doors slammed shut, leaving only Amanda and Mephistopheles all alone amid the cloaked figures lining the walls.

Mephistopheles crossed his arms as he looked down at Amanda who was still on her knees.

"Amanda, do you have any idea what you are?"

"I've been told more than once, yeah. I'm the Immortal Sin. Thanks for the reminder, Lucifer."

Amanda knew that she was pressing her luck but she didn't care.

Mephistopheles froze and glared at her before coming down to her level and looking her directly in the face.

"No one has called me by that name *since...*"

"*Since* you fell? Yeah, I know the stories." Amanda said and glared right back at him. "Such a shame."

"Don't you dare preach to me about shame!" Lucifer growled.

"Oh no, Mephistopheles, I can tell you all about it. Falling from grace is a Sin in itself for what *you* did."

He hissed in her face with anger but Amanda closed her eyes, refusing to look into his hateful soul.

"You have some nerve…"

Amanda couldn't believe it herself but the truth had to come out. She wanted to give him a taste of his own medicine.

"I guess I do."

"You know, it's interesting you would say that, given what your father is. Has he told you yet?"

"He's a Demon, big deal." Amanda said.

"He's not just any Demon. Do you see those standing all around the room?" Mephistopheles gestured to the cloaked figures who'd been stalking her.

"Yes. What about them?"

"Your father is one of them."

"What do you mean?"

"Well, let me first introduce you to the Seven Deadly Sins. Lust, Gluttony, Greed, Sloth, Wrath, Envy and Pride."

As he introduced them, they each seemed to step off their individual podiums and enclose the space a little tighter.

"You see, Amanda, since Acedia decided to show up here, it's all become very clear now. Years ago, when you were birthed unto the world, he disappeared. Vanished and it was all because of you. Because he committed the ultimate sin, the Immortal Sin and he decided to leave the Nine Deadly Sins."

Amanda looked around the room and counted the creatures along the walls.

"But there are only seven. Isn't that how it's always been?"

"No, not many know this but it all started with nine. Your father was the eighth and as for the ninth sin, Vainglory, she also disappeared and no one, not even myself knows why or where she is today."

Amanda recalled a brief conversation that she had had with Mitch a few months back, when they had first met. He had mentioned something about Sins dropping off the list but her memory was so vague she couldn't remember if he had said anything else.

Ace was a Sin, the eighth Sin and that was what the chant on that piece of paper must've meant.

Bring me to the darkest of my past, hidden in the shadows. Bring me to thy father, the eighth, my true and only blood.

Amanda realized that he must've risked his own life, his own safety from being hidden for so long to simply help her rescue Mitch.

He really did care about her. He wanted to help and he was risking it all to do it.

"But what does Acedia mean? What kind of Sin is that?"

"Acedia means carelessness, depression. You're father has truly proven himself of that. Pure carelessness."

It all made sense.

She wondered why he was always so sad, so depressed, so listless and his name was simply the answer. He was the definition of it all, if only she had known.

If it were the last thing she'd do, she wouldn't let anything happen to Ace, to the father she'd known who had chosen to help her regardless of the circumstances.

Amanda had no idea what to expect but there had to be a reason why he had lured her down there and it couldn't have been just to kill her.

"So, what do you want?" Amanda said impatiently. "Why did you bring me down here?"

"You know what? I am quite impressed with your attitude. You're definitely half Demon. I can sense more evil in you that you probably don't even have any knowledge about yet. There could be so much more, Amanda; so much power."

"Well, you see, that's where we differ. I'm not like you. I know that there's more to life than just power."

"But it feels good, doesn't it? I know you've had a hunger for power. All thanks to Malicious, you know how that tastes."

Amanda shook her head in rejection even though she knew that it was the truth.

"Amanda, we have more in common than you know. I was once an Angel, an Angel in the hierarchy of the Kingdom of Heaven. I was one of the favorites. I was practically a God, myself. But when things changed, I couldn't help myself. I was supposed to be His one and only favorite. I wanted it all and yet I bowed down to his glory. I know the struggle you're dealing with between the light and the darkness. And besides, I know what you want. I know what you crave, even through all of this."

"How would you know what I want?"

"I've been watching you. I know what you desire. You want an answer. You want to know why you exist."

Amanda was speechless because deep down in her heart, she had wanted the answer ever since she'd learned the truth.

"I know that you have been yearning to know why the Immortal Sin exists."

She couldn't resist the urge to know what he had to say.

Could he really know why she was there? Why she was created? What it all meant?

"Yes, I want to know." Amanda finally said.

"Your fate is to join me."

"What? You can't be serious." Amanda said in disbelief.

"You're the ultimate being, Amanda. You are stronger than anything that has ever been. Why do you think Malicious kept you a secret from me."

"That can't be true. If he would've known that, he would've told me. He told me that no one knew what my fate meant or could be."

"Did you ever consider that I might know?" Mephistopheles smiled and Amanda didn't know what to believe.

"I had thought about it, but I also thought that..."

"Forget it. The guy upstairs wouldn't know. If he'd have known, wouldn't you think he'd reach out and help you given how all powerful and all mighty he is thought to be? He would've helped you already and look at what he's done so far. Absolutely nothing. I want to give you that answer and he obviously does not. You're fate is to lead my army."

"Army?" Amanda asked, confused.

"When the world ends, my army will take over. The world as you know it will come to an end, and so will the Kingdom of Heaven." He hissed. "And in order to do that, I need your power, I need your strength. You will be unstoppable and put the pitiful world to its' absolute end with me and..."

"The Obsidian?" Amanda cut him off.

"Yes, The Obsidian. I guess Acedia has shown you quite a bit."

"No, just what's important." Amanda retorted.

He had been waiting for the Immortal Sin the entire time so that he could unleash The Obsidian on the world. He had been waiting for one thing to make him all the more powerful and Amanda refused to believe that her destiny meant just that.

He had simply wasted his time and Amanda was going to make that very clear.

"I won't do it." Amanda refused boldly.

"I'm sorry, what did you say?" Lucifer asked and Amanda could see anger building behind his ice cold eyes.

"I. Won't. Do. It."

"Well, that's a pity because I have some bad news for you. If you don't join me, then you can say good bye forever to your father and Malicious. You have no choice, Amanda. Join me or they perish forever into The Obsidian."

Amanda couldn't do it but she couldn't lose the love of her life and the father she had met for the first time.

Amanda knew that she couldn't fight with her White Light but she was after all in the Underworld and her darker side felt all the more powerful down there.

She knew that fighting fire with fire with the most powerful one from the source was pointless but it was worth a shot to save those that she cared about.

"Lucifer, your offer is tempting," Amanda said before looking up at him with anger behind her swirling, illuminated eyes. "But I'm going to have to refuse!"

A large burst of Hellfire ignited in her hands and she shot it directly at him, projecting it as fast and as hard as she could.

"The answer is No!"

It caught him off guard and he flew back into the shadows causing the building to rumble and shake from the impact.

Amanda expanded her wings and she quickly flew up into the air as she braced herself for the crash through the ceiling of the cathedral.

Ear piercing screams could be heard from inside the church and she could only assume that it was the Seven Deadly Sins reacting to her choice and the devastating blow to their king.

She hit the solid wall hard but managed to burst through the top and into the dark sky, hovering above the steep spires of the church.

She frantically scanned the environment, swooping down over the lit areas of the landscape in search of Ace and Mitch.

A faint yell could be heard from somewhere off in the distance and Amanda flew as fast as her wings would carry her through the sweltering air.

There wasn't any way that she was going to let Lucifer win and she refused to believe a word he had said.

All she knew was that she had to get Ace and Mitch out of there before the worst could happen.

Amanda flew in the direction where she heard the yell to find a group of Demons gathered near by a cliff.

Amanda landed hard on the dirt ground beneath her feet to see Ravish holding up Mitch's lifeless body by his throat over the cliff.

Next to her was Rabid and Lilith holding Ace by either one of his arms, threatening to toss both Mitch and Ace over the edge.

"Oh, how cute! Amanda's come to rescue her father and this pathetic excuse for a Demon!" Ravish said and squeezed tighter on Mitch's throat.

"Ravish, don't do this." Amanda demanded.

"The Obsidian awaits…" Rabid said hungrily. "And there's nothing you can do!"

"Ravish, let him go. Just take me instead. I deserve punishment for what I've done. Malicious has taken enough, he's done. Can't you see that? I'm the one you want." Ace said in defeat.

Ravish looked from Mitch to Ace, contemplating his point.

"No! What are you doing? You don't deserve this!" Amanda yelled at Ace, wondering why he was simply surrendering himself so easy.

"For once, Acedia, you're right. You are more valuable to her than this dead Demon."

Ravish threw Mitch to the ground as if he were a ragdoll. Amanda knew that Mitch wasn't dead and as long as she could somehow get out of the Underworld with both of them, everything would be okay but she had no idea how she was going to make that happen.

The wicked Demon walked over to Ace and got up close and personal with him.

"Are you ready for the end?" Ravish said, hissing at him.

"You're mistaken, Ravish. It's the end of you that I'd be worried about." Amanda said confidently.

"Oh, really?" Ravish said and raised her eyebrows with surprise as she turned away from Ace. "The end of me? You'd like to think that wouldn't you?"

"Yes. It's about time that your fun and games come to an end and I'll be the one to do it!" Amanda said and braced herself ready for a fight.

"We'll see about that. Let's see what you've got!" Ravish commanded as a burst of Hellfire violently flew out from each of their hands.

Amanda knew Ravish was strong and had a lot more experience with Hellfire than she did but she was determined to destroy Ravish once and for all.

The fire crackled and roared as Amanda tried to fight with every ounce of soul to not let evil overcome her or anyone she cared about.

"You won't win!" Amanda shouted above the roar as she struggled to maintain her strength.

"You're nothing but weak! You cannot beat me! Face it! You will lose! You will lose everything and anything you love if you don't join our army!" Ravish yelled back.

"No! I will not do it!" Amanda countered.

"Have it your way!" Ravish yelled and let out a massive wave of heat that caused Amanda to lose her footing and fall backwards onto the ground. "Say goodbye to your father!"

Ravish quickly turned around and lashed out with a furious swipe of her claws as Rabid and Lilith let go of him, causing Ace to fall backwards over the cliff toward the bubbling tar pit of The Obsidian.

"No!" Amanda cried and rushed to the edge of the cliff to grab him but his hand was no longer within reach.

Amanda stomach cringed at the thought of losing the only father she had ever known for a matter of less than twenty four hours. Despite feeling distant from him, he had given up everything to help her at her request and she refused to lose him just like that.

Amanda lunged out to fly when Lilith and Rabid grabbed hold of both of her arms so tightly that she couldn't even move.

"You're not going anywhere." Rabid sneered.

"Life isn't forever, Amanda. Death is forever. Think about it. When you live your life, it has an ending. And when you die, it's infinite. You will never see that someone again!" Ravish growled.

"No!" Amanda cried out desperately as tears rolled down her face. She was helpless to do anything but watch Ace fall to his death.

Chapter 31

SAVI⊕R

*A*manda felt as if her world had ended as she watched her father fall to his death.

She was helpless and it only reminded her of when she had fallen from the flaming rollercoaster and there was nothing she could do about it.

But within a blink of an eye, a blinding white light shot out from an unknown source and all of the Demons recoiled with agony as they all were thrown back from the tremendous explosion.

Amanda could hear horrific screams but she still could not see anything through the blinding light.

Had Nan come to their rescue again?

Once the light dyed out, Amanda peeked down over the cliff into The Obsidian but her father was nowhere to be found.

Was it too late?

Amanda noticed a light twinkling above her and looked up to find a glowing figure of a woman with enormous white wings and Ace's Demonic, lifeless body caressed in her arms.

The impact from the catch had knocked him out as he lay limp in her embrace.

The woman floated downward and landed on the ground next to Amanda.

"He's hurt from the light but he will be fine. He needs time to heal."

The Angel's voice was similar to that of Nan's, beautiful and pleasing to the ears, like the soft sound of wind chimes and bells.

Amanda didn't know what to say as she got back up to her feet and stared wide eyed at the angelic beauty.

"Thank you." Amanda said graciously.

The Angel's light was so bright that even up close anyone would barely be capable of determining what she actually looked like.

Amanda could only see that she had long blonde hair and beautiful crystal blue eyes.

"Amanda, I am proud of you." The Angel said thoughtfully with kindness and fondness in her voice. Amanda could only think of one other person that would say something so... motherly.

"Are you... are you... Serenity?" Amanda stuttered.

"Yes, I am. There is much to say and explain. We will talk once we leave this dreadful place. What is that down there? I have never seen that before." Serenity asked curiously as they peeked over the cliff together.

"It's something horrible."

"I could sense its evil. Please explain when get back to your world."

Serenity floated over to Mitch who lay on the ground, motionless and unmoved.

"Amanda, pick him up and we will leave here before Lucifer decides to act."

Amanda stopped before reaching Mitch and made a last minute decision.

"Hold on. There's something I have to do first."

"What are you doing?" Serenity asked.

Amanda didn't respond as she headed over to where all of the Demons writhed in agony from the impact of the arrival of Serenity.

Amanda found Ravish amid the other Demons and without any reluctance, grabbed the Demon by the neck and carried her effortlessly toward edge of the cliff.

Amanda could feel her own hatred and anger flowing through her veins and she wasn't letting anything stop her from doing what she thought was right.

Ravish was an imminent threat to her and everything and anything she cared about and Amanda wasn't going to let it happen any longer. No matter what Amanda did or where she went, she knew that Ravish would find a way to wiggle into her life somehow and she wasn't going to tolerate it, not when the lives she loved could be harmed.

Ravish garbled nonsense as Amanda squeezed the monster's throat tighter and tighter.

"You won't bother me anymore, Ravish. I'm done with you. Once I'm through with you, I can finally live my life with one less thing to worry about."

Amanda held Ravish high up above the cliff, threatening to drop her into The Obsidian.

"Oh, and I don't believe this is yours."

Amanda grabbed hold of Ravish's claw and slid off Mitch's ring before sliding it into the pocket of her ripped jeans.

Ravish growled and hissed with anger despite the crippling pain running through her beastly body.

"One last thing before you disappear forever. I just want to let you know that for once, you're right. About what you said about life and death. I will never see your face again."

Amanda let Ravish slide through her fingers and plunge down into the depths below.

Ravish's terrifying screams echoed throughout the canyon as she fell fast through the air but Amanda remained unmoved and indifferent.

The Demon splashed into The Obsidian, leaving no trace of her behind except boiling black sludge below.

She was gone.

For good.

Amanda walked back over to Serenity, feeling more distant from anything else than she'd ever felt before.

"Okay, *now* I'm ready to get out of here. Out of this Hell hole."

"What happened to forgiveness, Amanda?" Serenity asked as she watched Amanda take hold of Mitch over her shoulders once again.

"Someone once told me that forgiveness does not exist down here." Amanda said, reiterating what Ace had told her, even though she knew it sounded cold coming out of her own mouth.

"So I see." Serenity said and gently took hold of Amanda's hand as they lifted off the ground together and flew at the speed of light up and out of the Underworld.

Chapter 32

FAMILY REUNION

Exiting the portal was painful and Amanda started to feel herself change back into her human form. She could feel tugging on her hair as if the black was being ripped out strand by strand and her hooves altered back into human feet and toes.

The four of them burst up and out of the Grand Prismatic Spring, high into the air before floating back down to the Earth in the forest just outside of the spring.

Amanda had no idea how long they had been below but it was still day time and the sky was blue with puffy white clouds.

"It's best we stay hidden in the trees over here that way we go unnoticed." Serenity said as their feet touched the ground.

Amanda lay Mitch down in the grass and got down on her knees to find him transformed back into his human body that she had grown to love so much.

She tried to wake him with her kisses but his body was still in a comatose state and he was badly bruised and cut up.

"Why won't he wake up? Will he be okay? I know that he's alive. He said my name a little while ago." Amanda said, feeling nothing but worry for him.

"He should be fine. He needs time to heal and he's been badly beaten. His soul has been torn apart. It will take time to put itself back together, if it can."

"What do you mean, if it can? He might not make it?" Amanda said feeling frustrated with the uncertainty of the situation.

"He's a Demon, Amanda. There isn't much I can do and I only know so much about them."

Amanda looked up to find the magnificent vision of her mother gone and transformed into a tall woman with long blonde hair and dark eye makeup encircling her bright blue eyes.

Her skin was flawless and ivory white but she wore clothes that surprised Amanda for being considered an Angel.

Serenity wore a short black leather jacket with matching leather jeans and a white lace shirt. Her biker boots had a big silver buckle and the entire ensemble didn't remind Amanda of the original vision she had in her memory of her own mother.

"This is so weird. You don't look like anything that I expected." Amanda said and stood up as she looked her mother up and down. "How did you know to come help us?"

"The power of prayer. Your grandmother prayed, as well as your Watcher, Gregg and your new Watcher friend, Luca. I believe your human friend prayed as well. Your grandmother had formed a prayer circle and sometimes prayer is all you need."

That simple news made Amanda miss her friends and grandmother ten times more than she already did. She was more than thankful for the friends she had and the magnificent grandmother that stayed by her side and had saved her life once before.

Amanda looked up at Serenity confused when she noticed something unusual.

"But Nan said it's dangerous to go to the Underworld as an Angel. How did you manage to get there?"

"It's more than dangerous and we technically do not have the right to be down there but I needed to save the only two things that have meant the most to me. I also knew that it was the right time to finally step into your life. If there was going to be any moment at all, it was going to be that one."

Amanda could feel herself starting to get emotional and she could feel a lump forming in her throat.

She hadn't seen her mother in so long and the only memory she had was a phone call on her sixteenth birthday.

"I only know the sound of your voice. That's really all I've ever known. And here you are, in person right in front of me and it's still hard for me to believe. It's still hard for me to believe any of this." Amanda said trying not to cry. "Do you have any idea what I've been through? Not being able to see or speak to my parents, like ever? I don't even feel like I know either of you at all."

"I know, sweetheart. We have a lot of explaining to do." Serenity said with sympathy. "Please forgive us but we did it for your safety as well as our own."

"Amanda, hear us out." Ace said weakly as he got up slowly to his feet. He too was back into his human form, five o'clock shadow and all.

"Oh, I'll hear you out but first you have to tell me everything. I mean, everything. No mores lies, no more secrets. If we're going to try to be a family, that is not what it's about. It's about having a real father, a real mother and a trust between us. Period." Amanda demanded and crossed her arms as she waited for their explanation.

"Amanda, but," Ace went to speak before Serenity cut him off.

"No, she's absolutely right. Now that everything is out in the open, this is our chance to do what's right, regardless if what we did was right or wrong. If we want to make things right and learn to trust each other, we have to tell her what and why we did what we did."

Ace held his gut in pain before finally shaking his head in agreement.

"Where do we start?" Ace asked as he walked over to a large rock and sat down as gingerly as he could.

"Amanda, going back years and years ago, your father and I didn't meet on purpose. It was actually by accident."

"How far back are we talking?" Amanda asked.

"It started back during the Black Death. Or what you would know as The Plague that took over in Europe. It was a horrible, horrible time." Serenity explained and her tone of voice changed as if she weren't particularly fond of the memory.

"So, that would explain your accent." Amanda said out loud and looked over at Ace.

"Yes. It kind of stuck with me, I guess." Ace said before Serenity continued the story.

"As you can already guess, Demons are capable of many things, but they are also capable of creating and spreading the likes of horrific diseases that can kill, such as The Plague."

"Wait, are we talking like centuries ago?" Amanda asked.

"It started in the 1300's, I believe. It was so long ago." Ace said.

"You were alive then?" Amanda asked in disbelief.

"Yes, we are very old even though it may not look or seem that way, Amanda," Ace answered and Amanda stopped pacing.

"Whoa, whoa, so you're saying that what I learned in my history class about the Plague is all wrong too? It's all misunderstood because no one knows about the supernatural stuff, like Angels and Demons?" Amanda asked, growing more irritated by the thought of ongoing lies and deception of what she thought was reality.

"Yes." Serenity sighed.

"God! It's like everything I've ever known is fake. It's like an endless list of real life stuff turning into something completely different right in front of me!" Amanda said feeling the peak of her frustration before taking a moment to catch her breath. "Okay, I'm sorry, it's just hard to take in when what you thought you always knew wasn't true and it just keeps on going."

"I understand it must be hard." Serenity said sympathetically.

"Amanda, remember when I told you about the spring over there? And that it's not what it seems and we know better than all that crap? This is just another one of those situations." Ace said and cringed in pain as he tried to get more comfortable.

"Great." Amanda said sarcastically and started pacing back and forth as she tried to let it all settle into place. "Okay, then, so what happened next?"

"Well, a group of Demons were aboard a few ships that came into the port. During that time, Demons were on a killing spree in Europe, spreading The Plague everywhere and anywhere, killing millions of humans. They took pleasure in the millions who were living in fear and dying in vain. As you can guess, I was there with them when one night, and understand that I was very different back then. I was a monster, just like any of the other Sins. But then we ran into each other, literally. And after that moment everything changed." Ace said as he glanced over at Serenity and Amanda could see the care for her through his eyes.

"Yes. And I was sent over to assist in the many that were in need of me and arrived by boat late one night. I wore a dark cloak to conceal myself from anyone noticing that I was anything but human."

"But, what were you doing there if Demons were everywhere? And what do you mean that they were in need of you?" Amanda asked curiously.

"Sometimes our assignments involve risk and well, remember how I told you that I worked around the world for the Peace Corp? Well, obviously you know now that that's not true. But it was the closest I could come up with that could possibly define what it is that I actually do."

"Then, what do you actually do?"

"Well, my name is Serenity. My job as an Angel is to carry out exactly that. During The Plague, many people were suffering and dying. I would appear to them and grant them the gift of serenity and some peace of mind in order to help guide those poor souls to the light in order to pass on peacefully. Given my ability and the purpose I was as an Angel, I was and am of importance to the Lord and I am counted on to assist souls, to help guide them in the right direction. I'm here to reassure them that everything is okay when entering the Passage of Light."

"Passage of Light?" Amanda asked.

"You know when people have experiences with death, they talk about how there's a light that opens for them and they see it? Well, that's what that is and some people who have survived come back with a glimpse of it in their memory. It's the path that leads them down a tunnel to the gates of Heaven."

Amanda was speechless by Serenity's story and she just listened in awe.

"But going back to the Plague, Ace was there the night that I arrived to help those who needed me."

"I so happened to cross paths with your mother and the rest is history. I ran into her and when our eyes met, something changed in me. I was no longer the Eighth Sin and I had a new purpose. She had shown me that Light wasn't just harmful to me, but that it was capable of so much more. My life didn't have to be all darkness. I don't know what or how it happened but it did by some miracle."

Amanda thought of what Mitch had said to her many times before about how she had shown him more than he had ever known and it changed him because of the White Light within her. The story sounded all too familiar and it warmed her heart to know that she and Mitch were not alone in experiencing this… miracle.

"It might have been a miracle but we had to hide our affections from our worlds. No one could know because it would cause our ultimate fate to be unknown. We didn't know what would happen but here we are today. We managed to hide it all, even when we discovered that you were going to be birthed."

"But, wait. When did you find out that I was going to be born?" Amanda asked without trying to make the conversation too awkward.

"Well, if you think that you were conceived during the 1300's, you're wrong. It was about a century ago, just before the year 1900."

"What?!" Amanda asked, shocked with her mother's response. "Are you saying that you were pregnant for like... a hundred years?!"

"Well, your father and I didn't know what to expect. No one would think it was even possible but it was. This had never happened before and it was only spoken of through legends and myths. All we knew was that humans have a nine month cycle and obviously Angels and Demons don't have any such cycle. So, yes, it was a very long time period, but well worth it. We had to accept what simply just was."

"Holy crap..." Amanda said and held her head in her hands. "This is crazy. Just when I thought I knew everything I didn't know before, there's always more."

"You wanted to know the truth and what happened, so here it is." Ace said as he stood up slowly from the rock.

"I know, but this is just... I have no words. Keep going, don't mind me." Amanda insisted.

"Once you entered this world, we knew that the Earth, this human world was your sanctuary, your true home. You were born between two completely different worlds and the human world met right in the middle. It's why we think you have such beautiful green eyes." Serenity said thoughtfully.

"We also knew from what had been told that this being, this Immortal Sin would be the most powerful being among Angels and Demons alike. But the only thing that was uncertain was your future. Your fate. What your purpose in existing actually meant." Ace explained, "But as a result of being afraid of the consequences of whether any of us would be harmed or receive punishment for the actions that we committed, we decided to hide you in order to prevent anything that would possibly destroy the one object of our miracle that happened, you." Ace explained and took hold of Serenity's hand.

"We decided to separate and go into hiding, constantly moving from place to place to avoid any confrontation with other Angels or Demons looking for us. The only ones who helped us were Glory, who you call Nan or your grandmother and there was one last Demon who knew about it all…" Serenity said and glanced over to Ace, encouraging him to finish the story.

"Vainglory. She likes to be called Vanity rather than Vainglory but she is the other Sin, the ninth Sin that left the original Nine Deadly Sins other than myself."

"Mephistopheles mentioned her. She just left because you wanted her to?" Amanda asked taking a few steps forward, intrigued by the mystery of the last Sin.

"Vanity left because she wanted to help me. She was the only Sin closest to me and she had a better understanding of the situation I was in because she chose to pull herself away in order to help me. Sins usually travel together and she had been in disagreement with the way of things for a while so she chose to leave the Underworld with me. I have not seen her in years though." Ace said sadly before pointing out Amanda's necklace that was still strung around her neck. "She is the one who created that necklace I gave you. One night she combined some of her powers with mine and formed that pendant to resemble a tree representing our family. It obtains powers that easily enable you to reach out to me in your dreams, as Demons do when they communicate and form nightmares."

Amanda twirled the golden chain around her fingers and thought of what Mitch had told her.

"Mitch told me that Demons could create nightmares and when Nan gave me this, I knew it was true. I could actually see you for the first time in my life." Amanda said trying not to get choked up when she thought of Mitch still lying on the ground. "Mitch!"

Amanda knelt down and tried to wake him once more but he remained unconscious.

"What can we do? I need him and I didn't go through all of this just to see him die."

"Let's head back home and we'll figure out something." Serenity said as she spread her wings and offered her hand to Amanda. "Take my hand and I'll fly us all home. We will fly above the clouds so that we will not be seen."

Chapter 33

WELC⊕ME H⊕ME

*I*t was as if the journey home through the clouds only lasted a matter of minutes before the four of them descended upon the house that she recognized as home.

It must've been Serenity's angelic ability, her speed was incredibly fast and it was as if the sky was a blur the entire way home.

Ace, Serenity and Amanda gently touched ground on the front path before the porch to find Nan, Gregg, Luca and Alexia waiting for them.

"Thank God! We were all so worried! I'm so glad you're okay! It's been days!" Alexia said as she ran up to Amanda.

"Days?" Amanda asked and turned to Serenity and Ace with a questioning look.

"Time has different significance when you're in a different world. It might not seem that way, but it does." Serenity said.

"Is he alright? What happened?" Alexia asked, noticing Mitch resting against Amanda's back.

"He needs rest. He's badly injured and it's not looking too good. Amanda, take him inside to lie down." Ace answered for Amanda.

"Okay, come with me upstairs and I'll tell you what happened." Amanda said to Alexia as she started up the steps and inside the house.

Nan walked over to Serenity giving her a tight and welcoming hug.

"Welcome home. You did the right thing." Nan said and pulled away.

"I know. Thank you for calling me. I couldn't bear to lose either of them." Serenity sighed.

"The power of prayer is one of the most powerful things. Thanks to the prayer circle we formed, we were able to reach you."

"I got to them just in time. I could've lost both of them."

"Thank goodness that it didn't happen. Thanks to our extra help, it made our prayers all the more powerful." Nan said and gestured to Gregg and Luca.

"Thank you, Watchers." Serenity said and walked over to Gregg. "And as for you…"

"I'm sorry, Serenity. I was forced to break my vow. But understand that Amanda made a choice and I…" Gregg tried to explain as he knelt down one knee with his head bowed in shame.

"You did everything you could. But Amanda is stubborn and I am learning that as we grow now that we're together now. She gets that from her father." Serenity said and glanced back as Ace.

"What? What can I say? It's not my fault for once." Ace said with a guilty look on his face.

Serenity smiled and glanced back at Gregg as she helped him up to his feet.

"You have done your duty and I don't consider our vow broken. You have limits and you cannot follow her into the Underworld. She made a decision that was impossible for you to support. I am thankful for all you've done to protect and watch over my daughter and given the circumstances, it wasn't an easy task to carry out."

"Thank you, Serenity. I care for her as a brother would and thanks to my buddy here, she had some extra protection if anything had happened." Gregg said and wrapped his arm around Luca's shoulder, playfully punching him in his side.

"I have and will do my best to help. Watcher's stick together and I understand how important Amanda is to you; to us all." Luca said and smiled.

"Thank you, both of you." Serenity said graciously.

"So, this is Amanda's father?" Gregg said turning his attention to Ace.

"Control yourself, Gregg." Luca reminded him.

"I'll take it that he's not a fan of Demons?" Ace asked and walked up to the Watcher. "Well, I wouldn't expect it anyway. But don't worry, I'm not a threat. I am here to make sure Amanda is safe. I've risked everything now and I'm afraid there's no turning back for me."

Gregg glared at him as if he were deciding whether or not to believe him.

"Well, I'm going to be keeping a close eye on you. Father, fancy accent and all, I have known Amanda longer than you have and more importantly, I've been here for her when you weren't. So, just make sure you behave yourself. I've had my fill of Demons but I'll admit that I am glad Mitch is back, for Amanda's sake anyway."

"Understood." Ace agreed then smirked. "You've got some attitude, Watcher. I'm pleased to know that you care for her and that you're here to protect her from anyone, even if it's me."

"Exactly right. It's hard to trust anyone, now-a-days. I'm just doing my job and Amanda's become more than just an assignment; she's a friend, practically a sister."

"That's good to hear. You chose a decent Watcher, Serenity. I'm impressed." Ace said and turned to Serenity. "He's strong and stands his ground."

"Yes, he does. I couldn't have asked for a better Watcher to protect what we care about most." Serenity complimented Gregg, causing him to blush.

"Alright, everyone, let's get more acquainted inside where it's safer than out here in the open." Nan said, gesturing everyone to go into the house but as everyone headed up the steps, Nan stopped Gregg before he could reach the door.

"Gregg, a word please?" Nan requested politely, waiting at the foot of the porch.

"What is it, Nan?" Gregg asked as he walked down toward her.

Nan paused to make sure everyone had gone inside before she spoke.

"I understand that you care for Alexia, but what do you plan to do with her, now that everything has changed?"

"Well, what do you mean?" Gregg asked perplexed by the question.

"Serenity and Ace are back in the picture and I sense that things are going to get even more dangerous. I would assume that you would do what's right for the safety of Alexia. She has already been involved for too long and I think it's best if you left her alone and stopped risking her safety."

"Are you saying that I should convince her to leave? Do you mean that I should break up with her?" Gregg asked, fearing that his assumption was correct.

"Yes. I understand that you care about her but I think if you truly care about her life, it'd be best to force her out. You must remind yourself that she is fragile; she is human. Risking a human life in the situation that we're all in is extremely dangerous; it's unreasonable to keep her involved. Do you understand?"

Gregg comprehended the situation but didn't willingly want to do what Nan was recommending. She was right and he couldn't fight the truth. Alexia was the only one who didn't have the abilities they all had and her life hung in the balance if anything were to happen.

"I understand." Gregg confirmed but couldn't help but speak from his heart. "She means a lot to me."

"Then do what's right. If you want to protect her, she should no longer be involved." Nan said and lovingly placed a hand on his shoulder. "I understand that it's painful and you've grown very fond of her, but I'm afraid that things have changed and the risk is too great."

Gregg's brow creased as he thought hard about the advice Nan was telling him.

"Okay." Gregg said sadly. "It will be done. I will talk to her, just give me some time to prepare myself."

He could see that Nan wasn't necessarily content with the decision either but they both understood that her life could be lingering in the balance depending on the circumstances.

Anything could happen and Gregg didn't want to risk losing Alexia. It'd be selfish of him or anyone else to keep her involved when anything could happen at any given time.

Nan couldn't bring herself to smile but instead squeezed his shoulder tighter before walking past him and back into the house.

Chapter 34

A SH⊕T IN THE DARK

"So, let me get this straight. The Devil wants you to lead his army to start the apocalypse?!"

Alexia sat in disbelief at the edge of Amanda's bed while Amanda tucked Mitch under the covers.

"Yes. It was hard for me to believe too but then he threatened to kill Mitch and my dad if I didn't say yes."

"But you said no, right?" Alexia asked quickly turning to Amanda.

"Of course I said no."

"So, what happened next?"

"I kind of shot Hellfire into his face and flew out of there."

"Wait a minute. You threw a ball of fire into the Devil's face? You are ballsy, girl! I can't believe you did that! Was he pissed off?"

"I'm sure he was but I got out of there before he could do anything about it."

"Wow. Just... wow. I wish I could've seen it all happen." Alexia said.

"But after I got out of there, I found Ravish, Rabid and Lilith with Ace and Mitch. I got into a fight with Ravish and..."

"A fire fight?!" Alexia asked with her wide blue eyes.

"Yeah, a fire fight and she ended up throwing Ace, or my dad, over the edge and into The Obsidian but thanks to Serenity, or my mom, she caught him and she helped us get out in time before anything else could happen."

"Whoa, that's insane! The Obsidian thing sounds just plain scary. I wonder what will happen now because he was waiting for you all along. Do you think he would start the apocalypse without you?"

Amanda hadn't thought about it before and knew that Alexia's question was a vital one.

"Actually, I don't know. I guess he could? I still have to tell Serenity, err, mom about it."

Amanda had no idea how to answer that question and the more she thought about it, the more it made her worry.

"Well, your parents seem… nice. I have to admit though that it's still weird to know that your mom and dad are in the picture now. Is it weird to call them mom and dad?"

"Yeah, it's more than just weird. It's like calling these complete strangers that you just met your parents. But they explained everything to me and I guess I understand why they did what they did." Amanda explained as she sat down beside Mitch. "But we're all together now and I guess we have to start from the beginning."

"True."

Alexia watched Amanda look at Mitch and she could see the concern settling upon her face.

"Do you think he'll be okay?" Alexia asked.

"I don't know. I hope so. I'll do anything and everything it takes to make sure he's alright."

"You really love him, don't you?" Alexia asked as she watched her friend kiss the Demon's forehead.

"More than anything. If it weren't for him, I don't know where'd I'd be or if I'd ever known what I was." Amanda said with tears brimming at the edges of her eyes. "If I had known that this was going to happen, I wouldn't have forced him out again."

"You did what you had to do. Don't feel bad about it. He just didn't understand. I guess we just have to pray for a miracle that he'll be okay." Alexia said thoughtfully.

A faint knock came from the bedroom door as Nan peeked inside.

"Amanda, your mother and father would like to speak with you."

Amanda looked back at Mitch, reluctant to leave his side when Alexia took her hand.

She had never seen him look so destroyed, so dead and it pained her to leave him all alone.

"Okay, we'll be right there. Let's let him rest." Alexia said as Amanda looked up at her friend. "It'll be okay."

Amanda took hold of her friends hand as they left the room and followed her grandmother down the stairs.

———✥———

"What is it?" Amanda asked as she entered the living room to find Ace and Serenity on the couch while Luca and Gregg hung out in the foyer.

"I think it's time." Serenity said and stood up from the couch.

"Time for what?"

"Time for us to find some answers. Your grandmother has told me that you've wanted to know the purpose of your existence; if there's a reason for all of this, for what you are."

"Well, yeah, but how are we going to do that?"

"There is one place that we have yet to go after all of this; the other world to which you *also* belong."

"Heaven?" Alexia asked from behind Amanda.

"Yes. It couldn't hurt to ask for an answer from The Lord now that everything is in the open. It'd be risky but I'm afraid we don't have anywhere else to turn. It's our only chance to get the answer you've been wanting." Serenity admitted.

"When would we go?" Amanda asked anxiously.

"Well, now or as soon as possible. With the uncertainty of Lucifer's next move, we should try to act as fast as we can."

"Oh! I know what Lucifer's next move is! I never got the chance to explain. It's The Obsidian!" Amanda explained. "That big black thing that he was going to fall into."

Amanda pointed at Ace as he stood up and walked to Amanda's side.

"Mephistopheles created The Obsidian in preparation for the apocalypse."

"But nothing can break through the barrier trapping in the Underworld." Serenity countered.

"It can. It's infused with his White Light and no one knows what could stop it if it were ever released unto this world. He could've let it lose at any time but no one knows what he's been waiting for." Ace explained.

"I know what he's been waiting for." Amanda said quietly.

"What? Amanda, what did he tell you?" Ace said as he turned to Amanda.

"He's been waiting for me; the Immortal Sin. He told me that with me leading his army for the apocalypse, he would be the most powerful. He wants me to lead his army."

Gregg and Luca entered the living after overhearing the conversation with uneasiness written all over them.

"What did you tell him?" Luca asked.

"I told him no, that I wouldn't do it and that's when he threatened to destroy you and Mitch's life." Amanda said to Ace, looking him straight in his dark eyes.

"Why didn't I know about this; this Obsidian?" Serenity asked stepping forward.

"Angels wouldn't know, neither would anyone from the outside world. It's been kept a secret for a long time and not even all Demons know. I'm not even sure if Mitch knows about it." Ace explained.

"Then we must leave at once. The Kingdom of Heaven needs to be informed before it's too late. Can he unleash it without Amanda?"

"Yes."

"You're sure?" Serenity asked again.

"Yes. You must go before it's too late. As we all know, he is unpredictable and it'd be lethal to anyone and everything." Ace said sadly.

"Amanda, we must leave. We will find your answer and we have to go to tell this to our Lord."

"She's right, Amanda. You both must leave now." Nan said from the foyer.

"But haven't you been hiding from him? Aren't you worried about what would happen if he saw you again and knew what you did?" Amanda asked walking up to her mother.

"It won't matter. What's important is this Earth and that the Kingdom of Heaven be aware of it and ready for a fight. It won't matter what happens to me. I will gladly take punishment if it means saving everything else. This is more important than myself." Serenity said confidently. "Let's go."

Serenity headed for the door when Amanda stopped her.

"But what about Mitch? I can't just leave him here. Is there a way to save him? We don't even know if he'll make it."

"We can ask the Lord. You can ask him anything when we arrive. We'll see what can be done." Serenity said and rested her hand on her daughter's shoulder. "Amanda, say your goodbye's now. We are leaving."

Amanda turned around to see all the faces of the only family she'd ever known looking at her with worry in their eyes.

Amanda walked up to Nan and gave her a tight hug.

"Be strong, Amanda. You will be safe with your mother. I love you."

"I love you too, Nan."

She pulled away to see Gregg and Alexia standing to her side.

"Don't worry, we'll watch over Mitch. We'll take good care of him. Just, please make sure you come back to us, okay? I can't lose my best friend." Alexia said as she hugged her friend, almost refusing to let go.

"I'll come back. I promise." Amanda said, trying not to cry.

"Come here, you." Gregg said as he picked Amanda up in a bear hug. "Don't you worry about us. We'll be fine. All we have to do is babysit two Demons while you're gone, how hard could it be?"

Amanda laughed as Gregg winked at her playfully. She turned to Ace who stood next in line.

"You're mother knows what she's doing. I hope you get the answers you're looking for." Ace said as he leaned in for a hug and without hesitation, Amanda hugged him back as tightly as she could. He was her father and despite the past, he had proven himself how much he had cared for her.

Before Amanda raced up the stairs to see Mitch, she noticed Luca was missing from the room.

"Where's Luca?"

"I think he's outside on the porch." Gregg said.

Amanda wondered outside onto the porch to find Luca sitting in Nan's rocking chair.

"Luca? Are you alright?" Amanda asked as she approached him.

"I guess. It's just hard to see you go when you just got back." He said sadly.

"I know. I'm sorry, but I don't want to leave either. I just have to do this one last thing though."

"I understand." Luca said stood up to face her. "Listen, I need to tell you something."

"Okay, what is it?" Amanda asked curiously.

"This isn't easy for me to say but I really like you. I mean you're such an amazing girl or Sin or whatever. I just care about you a lot and I know it might sound strange because I've only known you for so long but I figured now would be the best time to tell you because I have no idea when you'll be back."

Amanda could see his cheeks blush with embarrassment but his eyes maintained locked with hers.

"I, uh, well…"

Amanda didn't know what to say.

"Listen, I know you care for Mitch and all, but I can't hide what I'm feeling anymore. It's too difficult for me to do and I've never felt so strongly about someone before. I guess I don't expect much in return but I just want you to know that I think you're perfect. The list of qualities that I love about you could go on forever." Luca said and gently entwined his fingers with hers. "Just be careful okay? We all love and care about you too much to see anything happen to you."

Amanda leaned forward and gave him a hug to replace the words that she couldn't manage to say.

The truth was that she cared about Luca but Mitch was the love of her life.

After a few moments, Amanda pulled away and glanced into Luca's flawless blue eyes.

"Luca, I care about you. I do. You've done so much for me and I can't express how thankful I am for all of it. You are a great friend but that is the most that I can offer you; a friendship. I don't want to hurt you and I don't want you to think that I don't care because I do. I need you in my life, like Gregg and Alexia. Will that be enough?" Amanda asked and waited patiently for his answer.

A smile appeared on his face, relieving her of the uncertainty of his reaction.

"Yes. A friendship is fine. I really meant it during the prom when I said you were beautiful. You are in every way. I hope you find the answers that you are looking for and we will be here waiting for you when you get back."

"You know as much as I regretted it before, I am so happy that Gregg called you."

"I think you have one more person to say goodbye to." Luca said and glanced toward the upper level of the house. "We'll watch over him, don't worry." Luca reassured her.

"Thank you." Amanda said smiling and looking back at him as she opened the front door to head back inside.

Chapter 35

FAREWELL

*A*manda opened her bedroom door to find Mitch still lying comfortably under the covers.

She walked over and sat down gently beside him trying to resist the urge to cry.

For the first time, she noticed Oreo sitting by his feet all on his own. It warmed Amanda's heart to see her dog finally warm up to Mitch enough to lay by his side.

Amanda leaned over and hugged her dog who licked her face before resting his head back down on the blanket.

"Mitch." Amanda said glancing over at Mitch. She was hoping that he would finally say something back to her but he didn't respond. "I have to leave. I'll be back, I promise but there's something that needs to be done."

Amanda felt a tear tumble down her cheek and land on her hand that rested on his.

"I need you to stay strong for me. I don't know if you'll be okay but I will do everything I can to make you better. I can't lose you." Amanda said as she lay herself down across his chest and hugged him tightly. "There's so much I have to tell you. There's so much going on and I wish I could just tell you all about it but it's up to you to heal right now. Just to get better. It hurts so much that I have to leave now when I just got you back."

She felt as if they were going to drag her out of the house, kicking and screaming because she couldn't bring herself to leave his side.

"Please... please..."

Amanda didn't even know why or who she was begging to but her heart told her that she should just have hope despite how hopeless she was.

"You'll be happy to know that Oreo is lying here with you. He must know how bad this all is. I wish I could hear your voice. I wish you were awake and I could see your eyes. I wish you were just... okay. God, I feel so alone without you."

Amanda cried into the blanket and just wished that she could feel his fingers running through her hair.

"Ace, Nan, Alexia, Gregg and Luca are going to watch over you, so I know you'll be in the safest place possible. God knows that you don't like Gregg and Luca," Amanda said with a light hearted chuckle, "but they are here to watch over you for me. They care because I care."

Amanda slowly sat up and wiped her tears with her hands.

"I don't know if you can hear me, but I want to let you know that... you were right. I shouldn't have pushed you out like I did. Only bad things happen when I do. This is all like some kind of punishment for pushing out the most amazing thing I could ever ask for. I know that love is a gift but I'm discovering that it's not easy; especially in our situation. I should've come up with some way to practice my light even with you in the picture. It would've been a challenge but I should've known better. Sometimes I have to learn how to deal with multitasking, I guess rather than taking one thing at a time. I don't know. I don't know if things would've been different or this could've been prevented somehow but I have you here right here, right now and that's what matters. I wasn't going to just let you... die. I love you. I won't let anything else like that happen to you. I will find a way to make you better. I don't care what it takes."

Amanda squeezed his hand and leaned in to give him a gentle kiss.

"I love you. And I'll be back. I refuse to say goodbye because I know that I'll be back. I promise. Okay?"

Amanda kept expecting to hear him answer but when he wouldn't, it just made her even more upset and disappointed. It was as if she were living a real life nightmare, the worst that there was.

"I'll be back."

It was so hard to let go of his hand but Amanda forced herself to stand up from the bed before she walked over to the door.

Amanda glanced over her shoulder to see him one more time before leaving the room and shutting the door behind her.

———✒———

"Are you ready?" Serenity asked as Amanda walked down the steps into the foyer.

Amanda sniffled and wiped her eyes as she tried to collect herself.

"Yes. I'm ready. Please keep him safe." Amanda said as she turned to face everyone.

"We will." Alexia said and smiled.

"I will cast a protective veil of White Light over the house to make sure no more evil will enter this house. No offense." Nan said turning to Ace.

"None taken." Ace smirked.

"I'm pretty sure that they will be coming after you and Mitch. I will make it as safe as I can. Excuse me." Nan said as she pushed past everyone to be the first outside.

"Okay then. Everyone, we will return in due course." Serenity said as she headed out the door

"Be careful and good luck." Ace said and Amanda could hear a sweet intonation in his voice as he followed them outside and watched them walk down the steps.

Nan had her arms outstretched wide, as bright light flowed from her fingers tips, creating an invisible dome around the house.

The light formed what appeared to be thin webbing surrounding the house and once it hit the ground, the barrier became invisible to the naked eye.

Once Nan had completed creating the barrier, she stepped back up onto the porch to watch her daughter and granddaughter take flight.

The entire group watched from the porch as Amanda and Serenity walk down toward the street.

"Stretch your wings and prepare for flight."

"I don't know if I remember how to fly."

"Impossible. Amanda, have faith and find the hope within your heart. It will help you fly. Focus." Serenity said turning to her daughter.

Amanda knew that her wings could not be seen but she could feel them aching from their lack of use as she expanded them as wide as she could.

Serenity jumped into the air, gaining height effortlessly with her beautiful set of pearl white wings. She flew ahead of her, waiting for her high in the sky.

Amanda closed her eyes and tried to concentrate.

She would find a way to save Mitch and she had hope that he would make it; that he would be alright.

She would find answers, the ones she'd been looking for and what better place to go than Heaven for what she needed.

They needed to tell God about The Obsidian and the insidious plans that the Devil had in store.

Have faith. Have hope.

"Fly."

The word floated out of her mouth like a whisper and Amanda burst up into the air and through the clouds following Serenity's trail through the sky.

Chapter 36

QUESTIONABLE REGRET

"Well, all we have left now is hope." Luca said after watching Serenity and Amanda disappear into the sky.

"Yes. We should all have hope." Nan said as she waved everyone to go into the house. "Let's go inside and I'll whip up something to eat for everyone."

"This should be interesting." Gregg said and glanced over at Ace.

"Gregg, I get the point. I am going to be watched like a hawk because it's your job." Ace said as he headed inside.

"It's not only my job, I'm doing it for Amanda." Gregg murmured.

As everyone headed inside, Gregg gently grabbed hold of Alexia's arm.

"Um, can we talk for a minute?"

"Uh, sure." Alexia said even though she'd been caught off guard. "What's up?"

Gregg watched to make sure everyone went inside when he noticed Luca stopped to wait for him.

"I'll be right there." Gregg said and nodded, giving him the okay to go inside.

"Alright."

Luca walked inside leaving only the screen door shut behind him.

Gregg took Alexia's hand and walked her down the steps to the foot of the porch.

"Is everything okay? Are you okay?" Alexia asked curiously.

"Well, I want you to know that I care about you. I care about you a lot but..." Gregg hesitated as he struggled to find the right words.

"But, what? What's going on?" Alexia asked and pulled her hand away from his.

"Well, I want to protect you but I just don't know if you staying here is the best way to do it." Gregg said hoping that she'd understand where he was going with the conversation.

Alexia crossed her arms, perplexed with what he was saying.

"I... I think that it's best... that you go home. I want to protect you and I think the best way to do that would be to keep you out of all of this." Gregg said and he could tell from her facial expression that she was hurt. "Please don't get upset. I need you to understand that I don't want you to get hurt if something were to happen."

Alexia looked away from him for a few moments before she spoke.

"Are you... are you breaking up with me?" Alexia asked and Gregg could hear the strain in her voice.

"No, well... yes. It's complicated."

"You don't want me here with you?" Alexia asked.

"No, Alexia. You know that I care about you. Just having you know everything that's happened and not knowing what the future could hold, whether it's good or bad, I don't want to risk you being directly involved with this. I think it's best for you, for me, for everyone that you go home and stay safe with your parents."

"I understand but I don't at the same time. I love you, Gregg. We've been together for a while and even though I found out the truth, I still wanted to stay with you. Even though you lied to me, I still loved you. I just find this hard to understand. I mean I know you want to protect me but it's too hard to just walk away like that."

"I know we've been through a lot and I'm sorry. I love you, I do. I know this is hard, I mean, it's the hardest situation we could be in and I just want you to be safe and sound. Out of harms way. I just don't know any other way of protecting you." Gregg apologized.

"Gregg, I want you to know that I love you. But I will go because I know you're trying to do the right thing. Bad things could happen and I completely get it." Alexia said. "I just hope you're pushing me out because you think it's the right thing to do and won't end with something bad, like it did with Amanda and Mitch."

"What do you mean?" Gregg asked, confused.

"This just reminds me of what Amanda did to Mitch. Pushing him out to have a balance but in the beginning it was to keep him safe from her White Light. Nothing but bad things seem to happen when they aren't together. I just hope that it won't be the same with you and I."

"It won't be. I know that this is the right thing to do. It's not forever, Alexia. I want you to understand that this is all a precaution. I want you safe. Not only for my own sake, but for Amanda's too."

"Does Amanda know about this?" Alexia asked.

"No, no, she doesn't. This is my decision and I did not talk to her about this."

He didn't want to risk her life and assuring that she was no longer involved seemed like the best thing to do.

He cared for her, he wanted her to stay by his side as she'd always done but his mind was already made up.

"Please let me know what happens and that Amanda is safe. Tell her to come visit me when she gets back. I'll want to see her and make sure she is okay."

Gregg nodded and looked away because he couldn't bring himself to look into her eyes that spoke nothing but volumes of upset.

Alexia approached Gregg and gave him one last kiss goodbye, not knowing when she would see him next.

"Please, just, be careful."

Alexia's spirit was hurt but she understood the importance of the situation.

She walked back into the house, grabbed her purse off of the dining room chair and back out the front door, passing Gregg without another word spoken.

Chapter 37

A SURPRISE VISITOR

G regg shut the front door behind him and made his way over to the couch instead of sitting with Ace, Luca and Nan at the dining room table.

Luca watched his friend slump onto the couch as if something were wrong and he could tell something wasn't right.

Luca excused himself from the table and headed over to the living room.

"What's wrong, buddy?" Luca asked as he knelt down to Gregg's level. "Why did Alexia leave?"

Gregg sighed and looked his friend in the eyes.

"I let her go."

"Why? What happened?"

"It's just not safe for her here. Nan explained that it's too dangerous for her to be hanging around and she's right. So, I told Alexia to go home. She thinks I broke up with her, but I never said that. I just want her to be safe." Gregg explained sadly.

"Okay, well, I'm sure she'll be alright. I think you did the right thing."

"Well, she said something to me that got me thinking."

"What'd she say?"

"She told me that what just happened between us is similar to what happened with Mitch and Amanda. And look where they are now. It's just making me wonder that no matter what kind of decisions we make, that sometimes there isn't any way of preventing them from happening."

Luca sat down beside Gregg and placed his hand on his shoulder.

"Anything can happen at any time. Yes, God may have a plan, but we also make our own choices that determine that plan. Sometimes things happen and no one would have any way of telling what could have prevented them."

Gregg smiled and glanced over at his friend.

"You always know what to say. You know, it's kind of corny." Gregg laughed as Luca playfully punched his side.

"Whatever. Hey, if it weren't for me, you'd still be sulking over it." Luca teased as they got up from the couch when a knock on the front door surprised everyone.

"Who could that be?" Nan asked.

"I'm not sure." Gregg said as he walked over and opened the door to see a person in a dark cloak standing there.

Gregg braced himself, ready for a fight when the person lifted her hood.

Long dark hair flowed down the front of a fresh faced, exotic beauty with big black eyes.

"Who are you, Demon? What do you want?" Gregg asked cautiously when Ace forced his way between the Watcher and the mysterious woman.

Nan stood up from the table in shock.

"A Demon? How did she make it past my light?"

"You're here." Ace said in disbelief, ignoring Nan's question.

"I thought it was about time." The Demon smiled thoughtfully at Ace.

"You know, I don't think Serenity would be too happy about this." Luca said from behind Gregg.

"Don't be ridiculous. She has every right to be here as we do."

"How did she break my barrier?!" Nan demanded.

"Nan, like myself, Sins may not control the White Light but we are infused with some of it from Mephistopheles himself. It may not be much but it was obviously capable of letting her break through it." Ace explained and looked back at the mystery woman.

"Maybe we should up our defense somehow." Luca said nervously.

"Sin or no Sin, who is she?" Gregg asked, refusing to let down his guard.

"Her name is Vanity."

Chapter 38

DAWN OF THE NORTH

The sun was setting and Amanda couldn't help but be mesmerized by its extraordinary colors that blended into the sky.

It had been minutes since they'd left and already, Serenity and Amanda were flying over the Arctic.

"It's beautiful up here but it's definitely way too cold!" Amanda yelled loudly and held onto herself.

The icy wind brushed against her entire body and her hair flapped about in the wind, distracting her from enjoying the stupendous view from above.

Serenity flew in closer beside Amanda as they both sped rapidly through the brisk air.

"I know it's cold but just bear with it. We are almost there."

"So, Heaven is in the Arctic?" Amanda asked.

"Of course not, but the main entrance is."

"The pearly gates are in the Arctic?!" Amanda asked again. "I don't know if I can stay too long before freezing to death."

"Be patient and you will see."

The sun continued to set and the fiery sky was gradually turning into a blue-green as the stars started to sparkle their way into view above them.

"Stunning, isn't it?" Serenity asked as she watched Amanda admiring every bit of the landscape.

"It really is."

"This world has so much beauty and grace. Remember that it's your sanctuary, your home; as the Kingdom of Heaven is mine." Serenity said smiling.

Amanda smiled back but she couldn't help but wish Mitch was there to see it all with her.

As they flew on, Amanda noticed strange lights in the sky ahead of them.

"What's that? Is that…"

"The Northern Lights? Yes. Phenomenal aren't they?"

"Wow!" Amanda said in awe.

"It means we are here."

Amanda glanced over at her mother confused.

"Heaven is in the Northern Lights? It's in the atmosphere?"

"Not, exactly. You see, Heaven is its own world surrounding this world as you know it. The Aurora Borealis means the dawn of the north. It is where all the winds, north, south, east and west blow towards. The dawn of the north is the main portal into Heaven, and it is here."

"Are there other ways into Heaven too?"

"Yes, but only Angels can access them. I will explain more when we get there. Hold on tight!"

Serenity took hold of Amanda's hand as they flew faster and faster toward the lights.

The closer they flew toward them, the more rays of light started to show up and they started to come in waves, forming an empty space that was starting to fill up with White Light.

Amanda and Serenity flew up and into the portal and Amanda closed her eyes as they entered into the blinding light.

Suddenly, it was silent.

"Amanda, open your eyes."

Amanda obeyed her mother's command and opened her eyes slowly, unsure of what she would see before her when she heard her mother refraining a brief and familiar saying.

"And it shone with the glory of God. Its brilliance was like that of a precious jewel, like a jasper, clear as crystal."

Amanda stood speechless beside her mother, looking at the massive gates before her and the awe inspiring landscape that was unlike anything she'd ever seen before.

"The city had no need of sun or moon to shine on it, for the Glory of God gave it light."

Serenity gently took hold of Amanda's hand once again and smiled warmly.

"Amanda, I welcome you to the Kingdom of Heaven."

Epilogue

*A*lexia shut the front door of her house as she raced up the grand stair case in the foyer.

She was still having a hard time comprehending not being involved with what was going on.

The thought of being away from Gregg just made her even more upset and all she wanted was to jump onto her bed and cry herself to sleep.

"Alexia, darling, are you home?"

She could hear her mother call from the kitchen but Alexia was too upset to go see her.

"Yes, I'm home!" Alexia called out into the foyer as she headed up the stairs for her room.

She leaned against the door, dropped her purse and slid down it as she broke down in tears again.

"I love him!" She sobbed. "God! Why can't things ever be easy? I wish Amanda were here."

As she continued to cry, she tossed herself onto the silky comforter of her bed, nuzzling her face into the pillow.

Alexia curled up into a ball and tried to make herself comfortable because she knew that she wasn't going to move from her bed for a while.

Outside, a pair of maniacal, black eyes peered in through the bedroom window as the psychotic Demon watched her every move.

"This is beyond perfect."

The voice said hungrily in the shadows.

Rabid pulled over the hood of his leather jacket before rubbing his hands together vigorously with pleasure.

The Demon licked his lips as an evil grin crept across his face.

"An eye for an eye, Amanda. You take Ravish, I take *her*. The end is coming and you better be ready."

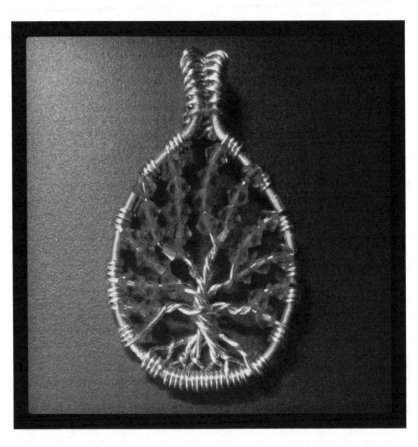

The final installment of The Immortal Sin Trilogy

Book 3

Coming in 2014

WILL EVERYTHING COME TO AN END

OR WILL A NEW BEGINNING DAWN?